I0589221

Pie and Whiskey

by

Stella Wallace

For Tona

The mornings always hit Emma the hardest, petitioning her to routinely convince herself that everything was going to be all right because nothing was as bad as she imagined. Dragging her dead weight out of bed, the reluctant departure from blessed slumber was met by the searing pain in her head generated by a brand of drinking that would bring grown men to their knees, the manner of which inclined no end. Emma Montgomery, a best-selling author, had once again hit a hard wall and no longer possessed the sheer will needed to climb over it. Her shining accolades as a young and up-and-coming writer, the talk of the town, had soured with each failed attempt, her agent-turned-boyfriend held first her hands then her breasts, there to sacrifice his time to coddle the young writer into delivering her next big thing. She took his advice and advances in stride because she had grown lonely, but more importantly, she refused to give up on her beloved craft. Her devout commitment to writing by itself, however, could not supply her with enough real content on its own and her impotency to search outside of herself due to fear of failure each day left her blankly ineffective. She lost touch with her friends, opting for the temporary drinking buddies found in local bars because at least they didn't judge her. With each passing year, she was falling short and feeling like a hack. She drank and drank to mask the presence of failure lurking in every corner, lying quietly in waiting and at the ready to pounce and maul her attempts at writing, laughing maniacally at her every defeat. She had yet to turn thirty years old and already she felt washed up.

Today, she fumbles her way through a simple trip to the bathroom. Everything hurts, making the going slow. She curses a lot. She aims for the kitchen to make some coffee, but beelines instead back to the purgatoric comfort of her big, soft bed. Her spacious loft in Downtown Manhattan makes it easy to navigate from one area of her living quarters to the other, and being a bit of a claustrophobe, she appreciates the high ceilings and open area. At least, she thinks, I can breathe in here.

Falling face forward into the creamy bedding, she hears the street level buzzer ring and groans. She hoists herself back up and without opening her eyes, feels her way to the plastic-faced intercom, landing a finger on the call button. "Who is this?" she bleats out, cranky is her new morning norm.

The voice is Latina, compassionate but stern. "Emma, this is Esther. I'm here to do your makeup, remember?"

Emma's eyes pop open, staring off into nothing. "Holy shit! Is that today? Ah fuck!" She buzzes her in, peels off her silk robe that has become her second skin, unlocks her front door, and sprints for the shower.

The long, stark hallway is filled with bodies milling about, everyone on a mission. The set of live television always pops with anticipation and possibility, the clock demands it, and this day is no different. Success of the show depends on those behind the scenes to be diligent and effective. And the Today Show is a prime example of a tightly run machine.

James Scott is already having a bad day and doesn't need anything to make it worse. He learned long ago that in order to become a successful agent, you had to become a cutthroat bastard first. He set his mind to that very thing and the success he was promised followed. At twenty-six, he was one of New York's top literary agents. Now, at forty-five, he is just as mean and ruthless as ever, a real my-way-or-the-highway kind of guy.

The show's assistant producer leads James to the green room. Once inside, he sees that Emma has not yet arrived and reaches for his cell phone, pacing and cursing under his breath. The call is not answered. He hangs up, annoyed.

The thin, Hispanic woman moves quickly to make Emma look less like the train wreck she is and more like an award-winning author. She checks her watch repeatedly, clucking her tongue with each new update. Emma sits bleary-eyed in her chair, ignoring her ringing home phone in the background. She knows damn well who is calling her, and has no interest in being reprimanded. "I don't want too much on my eyes, Esther. This is a morning show, not a quinceañera."

Esther exhales loudly. "Your eyes are all puffy, Mama. I can only do so much!"

"Let me see a mirror," Emma reaches out her hand blindly.

"I'm not finished yet!" Esther begins moving more quickly.

Emma covers her face with her hands, refusing any more paint. Esther sighs loudly and forks over a hand held mirror. Emma peers into it and shrieks, licking her fingers and rubbing them over her eyes, trying to fix the damage that's been done and creating more of a mess. "This is all wrong! I look Asian!"

"Stop touching it! Mama, you need to relax. You want me to put on a pot of coffee?"

"No, fix me a drink. Seven and seven." Emma puts down the mirror, closes her eyes and takes a deep breath. She opens her eyes and Esther has not moved, a salty expression on her face. "What the hell, Esther? Don't give me that look! I don't need your approval!"

"I'll get you just the one. But we gotta get going!" Esther shakes her head as she moves towards the kitchen area of the loft, searching for the contents.

"The glasses are below the sink. Three ice cubes. Soda's in the fridge, whiskey's on the counter, can't miss it."

Esther quickly mixes the drink. She returns to find Emma peering into the mirror again, spitting into a tissue manically and effectively wiping away the look that Esther has worked so hard at achieving.

8

Emma is growing hysterical, "Why would James book this? I can't be seen like this! I look terrible!" She grabs at the glass Esther is holding and downs half of it.

In the quiet of the green room, James continues to pace. The assistant producer of the show knocks lightly on the door, stopping James in his tracks. "Mr. Scott, is Emma here yet? It's 7:30 and we need to go over her spot. It's getting to be that time."

"I'm sure she's on her way. I'll ring her again," James turns away from the concerned assistant producer, exasperated, and dials her number again.

Emma sits calmly in the chair, drink in hand, while Esther works quickly on her face to repair the damage. The phone rings again, this time James leaves a message on her answering machine, his voice echoing in the cavernous room. "Emma, you were supposed to be here by now. They're asking for you. What am I supposed to tell them? I hope this means you are on your way. Don't you dare try to pull something here, Emma. Goddamn it!" Gone were the days of slamming a phone down onto it's cradle for desired effect, but Emma knew if he could achieve that same effect right now with a cell phone, he would have. She had been sleeping with James long enough to know when his anger transcended mere disappointment in her.

Emma's cell phone rings from across the room and she makes no motion to pick it up either. She continues to fidget uncomfortably as Esther struggles to keep her still. Emma grows more and more restless in the chair and resists the brushes so close to her eyes. Esther's cell phone rings. She pleads with a look. "Let me answer the phone. Tell him you're coming. It will give us both more time," Esther begs.

Emma rises clumsily from the chair, drink clutched. "Forget it. Tell him I'm in the bathroom. I don't feel good. Tell him I'm getting sick."

Esther answers her phone. "Hello, Mr. Scott... Yes, she's still here... I don't think she feels so good."

James screams into the phone. "Put her on the fucking phone!"

Emma plops down on the couch, eyes closed, remaining motionless. Esther tries to get her attention, to no avail. "But Mr. Scott, I think it's her stomach. Maybe if she just gets it out..."

"Is she drinking?" James asks through the phone, incredulous. "Esther, you listen to me. You get her here, or none of us will work again. You hear what I'm saying to you? No trabajo!"

Esther hangs up the phone and carefully approaches a despondent Emma. "Mr. Scott is really mad. We have to go. We'll do your face in the car."

Emma curls into a ball. "I can't, Esther. The book is awful."

Esther sits beside her, moving her hair from her face. "Your book is wonderful! What are you talking about? Your fans love you. ¡Vámonos de aquí!"

"I'm not going. I can't. You don't understand. It's humiliating being seen like this." The home phone rings again. Emma groans loudly, fishing for the receiver under the couch cushion. She takes a big swig from her drink and answers coyly, "Hello Bellevue."

James's voice barely contains his fury through clenched jaw. He speaks slowly and deliberately into her ear. "When I left you this morning, you were fine. What the hell happened?"

Emma sighs loudly. "I'm not fine, James. If you could see anything but yourself in all this, you'd know that. I'm sick. It's hard enough just to get the will to leave the house anymore, let alone face public scrutiny."

"Goddamn it, Em! They are throwing you a life preserver here, and you're swimming away from it! What the hell is wrong with you? I pulled in favors for this!"

"Fuck you, James. My new book sucks. You know time frames choke me and yet you forced this publication on me and now we both are suffering the consequences together. Let me write what I want to write and leave me the fuck alone," she hangs up the phone with rancor.

The assistant producer pokes his head in the room as James stares at his phone in disbelief. He recovers quickly when he notices the producer, fumbling for the right words to say. "I... I just spoke with her driver. The car got rear ended on her way uptown. Emma's a bit shaken up. She's going to go to the emergency room for tests. I apologize. I hope we can do this at another time. Excuse me." James lowers his head and briskly walks out.

Chapter 2

The afternoon sun makes Emma squint as she stumbles home in a stupor. A large group engaging in conversation convenes in front of a small church on the Bowery, smoking cigarettes, palming cups of coffee, and effectively blocking her path. Emma, operating in a haze, tries to pass. A young, pockmarked man with dyed, jet-black hair flicks his cigarette into the street and turns quickly to re-enter the building, bumping into her hard and knocking her over. She yells out in pain. "Son of a bitch! Watch where you're going, asshole!"

"I'm sorry, Ma'am. I didn't mean to," he replies sheepishly, trying to help her up.

Emma struggles to get up. "Ma'am? Do I look like one of your mother's friends, you fucking twat? Fuck off!" she rises, scowling.

A beautiful young woman wearing a green army jacket and jeans steps out from the building. Her straight hair is long and brown and she wears no makeup. She gently approaches Emma.

"Are you ok? Jimmy can be such a klutz," the young woman offers her a hand for support.

"What fucking difference does it make?" Emma's words slur as she brushes herself off.

"I'm Teresa. Why don't you come in and have a cup of coffee? It's good. I make it myself," Teresa gestures towards the door.

"What is this, fucking AA? I don't need any. Thanks."

Teresa looks at her with compassion. "You're that author, aren't you? Who lives in Soho?"

"Don't make me sorry I left the house."

"Hey, no one's judging you. I loved your first book! You should be proud of yourself. No one around here's done anything like that."

"You mean hold down a job?"

"I used to drink a lot, too. To kill the pain. It wasn't that I needed to escape the fact that I chose to sell my body for money. My choices were my own and I'd make them all over again. I think I did it because men continued to disappoint me on a heart level," Teresa sighs. "I'm guessing we're a lot alike. Please know you're not alone. There's always someone to talk to."

Emma shakes her head sadly and hobbles away. Teresa watches her go. "You know where to find me!" she shouts at her back.

"Noted," Emma mumbles with a half wave, not looking back.

After fighting with the front lock, Emma drags herself to the kitchen sink and methodically splashes water on

14

her face. She pours herself a tall glass of Jack Daniel's
with ice and sits down heavily at her desk. She lights up
a cigarette and begins typing furiously at her laptop.

~~Out From Under~~
Mistaken For Trash

1. Way In

She considered it her duty to evoke
pleasure, nearly culling the moniker
"Sister Teresa" inspired by the
missionary herself, any likeness between
the two found in mere traces of a
lifetime of service shared. Teresa
decided against donning the name, bowing
out of her silent salute to a woman who's
very essence was defined by her
selflessness, and injected her own brand
of dark humor over the matter by
settling on a more appropriate game
name, Trick, albeit an obvious one, and
the joke certainly wasn't lost on her
clientele. Every round of drinks brought
smiles, her beguiling way just a hair
removed, put the monster at ease. Proud
was he to make the bold female wanting.
The truth was her Trick was a process
and she enforced learning every step of
the way. She wanted to be good at this.

Growing up was an inconvenience. Everybody got in the way of her figuring out the direction her life should take and her proposed journey seemed too long an explanation to offer as a young person "on the verge". She learned early on that men leave. Physically, emotionally, and financially, her father had let them down, her mother forced into holding the disappointment card close to her chest indefinitely, the path to alcoholism eventual. The stubborn nights of debauchery by her own hand bled together, relinquishing health and hygiene in the absence of a man who only cared about himself and his trysts with those who gave him a mere second sideways glance. That well-worn path to self-destruction taken by sensitive types to fill the quiet of a day's end, to the point of nightly delirium, had the unfortunate effect of stinging those nearest the field of view. On occasion, Teresa would watch, stunned, as her soft, round mother, once lithe and exquisite, bounced off walls of a doorframe misjudged, shuffling blindly on her way to the kitchen to refill her cup with poison. Worse, she once had to peel off the kitchen floor in a back-breaking maneuver her saturated, broken-hearted, prematurely aging parent to then navigate her to bed in her day clothes because the effort of changing her into something more comfortable was too much to manage after the betrayal she felt being forced to bear witness to such a crime against one's self. Her mother was dying by her own hand, killing herself, because she felt she was to blame for her husband falling out of love with her. In truth, it wasn't loss of love at all, but her father's inability to deny carnal impulses and stay loyal to one woman. Her mother had siblings, but they were distant and the distance grew with each passing year. Friends were hard to come by when you were the type to lock yourself away because friendship takes work. Without a support system, her mother suffered tremendously. The case was clearly beyond a young girl's jurisdiction.

After such shiny examples, Teresa knew that loving a man would be impossible to do because who wanted to be made to feel that way in its inevitable wake? She only knew that love had an expiration date. No guarantees. This realization brought her no grief; the fracture was laid rest well enough inside her. She simply answered to no one. Her ailing mother would be on the receiving end of whatever love she would dare relinquish to anyone, but only when it could be spared. She hated being so harsh on the ailing woman, but Teresa felt larger than life with a fiery mind of her own. She embraced the discovery of self through trial, and welcomed the errors in stride. She had to. No one was going to be able to take care of her but her.

At fifteen, the other girls already had their run-ins with prospective male counterparts. Teresa met no such equal. The boys were nice enough, but hardly much to wave a stick at. The teasing only made their chances at landing a date with her worsen. Weasels, she thought, the lot of them. It was pressure enough accelerating beyond the learning curve, and the scholastic accolades that followed. But it was on that fateful day when she attended the wake of one such weasel who had wrapped himself around a telephone pole after a drag race outside of town, that she was able to truly appreciate their profound ineptitude. "Get up. You look ridiculous," her words chopped through the air above his still frame in that box for bodies of the done

18

and gone. The sneer on her face did not apologize and was misdiagnosed by the band of elders present as grief. Inside, she secretly contended with the notion that he'd never walk again, never ever be able to make fun of her for being beyond the scope of the adolescent dating game. He was stupid enough to die.

There wasn't much any boy could do right by her. Boys were interested in her, sure, despite her refusal to wear makeup and donning her signature green army jacket every day. But she would shame them because they weren't good enough and pity came easy. They failed to appreciate her dedication to herself and her extravagance as a thinking beauty. Shouldn't the boys go elsewhere and play? Where were the true contenders, the men? In her mother's words, meant to make her laugh but said in all seriousness, "Boys are stupid. Throw rocks at them". The tiny window she scarcely deployed shut tight when any guy she met failed to produce a burning passion comparable to her own. The prerequisites she instigated were construed to allow for only the best of everything, resulting in her spending most of her time alone. However, she never experienced loneliness. There's a difference, she concluded, when you like the company you keep by yourself. In that regard, you're never lonely. She counted the days until she could evacuate the premises, thank the mother figure for her valiant efforts, and get on with it. Teresa needed to stretch her long legs.

Mostly, she read. Her textbooks were always the first to go at the start of the school year. That way she didn't have to show up for class. She was always in attendance, in fact she never missed a single day, but used the time to sit and figure other things out. Her fellow students fascinated her in their delayed evolutionary stages. In the end, the ones she couldn't for the life of her peg down were the unmotivated types who wanted nothing more than to stay in town and collect tickets at the local movie house. What was the thought process there? It was such a foreign concept, one she could never get underneath. How could anyone want so little out of life?

One experience she carried with her every day was something so curious it took up quite a bit of her free time, mulling over its implications. She had gone out one Saturday night to a local club with a crew from school. Everyone got jacked up on vodka from a flask and

20

because she always refrained, she maintained a sense of control and could watch others from afar as her cohorts laughed and cavorted into balls of stupidity. Like a private investigator, she would gather information on the ways of the world that were currently made available to her from the so-called "cool crowd", in order to make stronger choices as to how to represent herself properly in the real world to follow. She never stooped to the level of her peers, but always sought to elevate herself to those older and savvier than her.

The Den was once a car garage next to a junkyard and it took them a while to get there because it was way out in the middle of nowhere. You had to know someone to get in if you were underage. It was the place everyone at school talked about because the music was cutting-edge industrial and it was almost impossible to get into and you had to wear all black and be hardcore and oh-my-god hate your parents. Teresa wore the same green army jacket as always and didn't hate her Mom, not really, so she was further removed with regard to any true peer involvement, yet she went just the same. Her mother thought she was elsewhere, and the defiance inside that innocent lie young people tell was exciting enough to get her through any second-guessing of whether or not tagging along was a good idea. The rebelliousness felt good. Plus, she wanted to know what the fuss was all about.

It was as dark and intimidating as they had described, full of young people on their way to becoming dangerously intoxicated and inevitably in trouble with their parents when they were dropped off well past their disregarded curfew, to be left behind on their front lawn with a shirt covered in vomit, a deficit of excuses. Everywhere she turned, drama ensued. In one corner a pretty girl was trying to revive her friend who had been knocked out while slam dancing. Another couple was engrossed in an argument that appeared on the verge of becoming physical, apparently because the girlfriend was caught kissing some other boy.

As Teresa moved through with nonchalance she garnered interest from some of the regulars, bikers with beards and thick boots and attitudes that were beyond what she could possibly handle at seventeen, but she didn't dare act like it. Her indifference to their gazes created reactions that tickled her sensibility as a woman-to-be. She waited for an opportunity to set a stride here before she found her ride home. As she felt her way through a dark hall that led to the back room, it was a female voice above all else that caught her attention. The voice commanded the floor. She searched and landed on the black haired beauty dominating from behind the bar. She moved closer to get a better look at the bartender, who spotted her stare through the smoke. Ignoring the incessant demands for more booze, she looked directly back at Teresa as though she were the only other person in the room, devouring her in a way that made Teresa tremble to be seen. This woman immediately made her feel how special she was. Her full lips parted and gifted her with a delicious smile and it suddenly dawned on Teresa she wanted more from this woman, whatever could be afforded. The bartender surprised her further when she jumped over the bar, despite the hollers from thirsty patrons, and headed directly towards her.

"Who are you? I haven't seen you in here before. What's your name?" she touched Teresa's face with a long forefinger, then sufficiently shocked her by reaching in and kissing her deftly on the mouth. It was wet and undeniable and totally unbelievable. Teresa succumbed with a moan that came from deep within, despite herself. It was pleasure without thought, free of any worry, and she moved her tongue in line with the soft-mouthed chaos that was this moment.

"Trick," she said when there was a moment to speak.

"What kind of name is that?" the beauty laughed in her face and kissed her again before she could speak any further.

When she pulled away, face so close as to steal breath, Teresa muttered, "I made it up," feeling young and embarrassing, but holding her ground.

"Teddy! The whip!" the beauty hollered to the bouncer standing at the exit and before Teresa knew what was happening, she was told to stand against the far wall with everyone looking on and jeering. At that moment, she chose not to care, because this woman was the object of her total affection. She buried her face in the wall, palms flat on the cold, concrete wall, her body expectant of anything. She squeezed her eyes shut, then thought to open them long enough to

24

peer from side to side, looking for the kids from school she had come to this crazy place with, hoping not to lock eyes with any one of them. She felt the slightest sense of relief over the fact that the room was filled with unknown faces, heralding grown-up expressions that supplanted what had once made them lovely children. She figured she was safe enough from detection, that her friends were in the main room having their fun in the notorious mosh pit and wouldn't catch frightful site of her participating in this strange ritual for the sake of the bar beauty who, at this point, could have absolutely anything what she wanted.

The leather cracked sharply across her back and what she felt through her shirt actually aroused her. The whole episode didn't last long, the party spectacle that she had become was sufficiently actualized, and through the raucous laughter, Teresa got a parting kiss from the bartender, who introduced herself as Barbara and handed her a phone number through the confusion. Teresa skipped away, somehow content, to look for her friends to demand that it was time to go home. She wanted to be alone to replay the events of the evening in the silence of her bedroom and then to sleep as quickly as possible in order to get tomorrow underway. Because Barbara had told her in parting that they were going on a date. And Teresa couldn't bring herself to think of anything else.

The next day was completely eclipsed by images and thoughts of how she would touch the different parts of Barbara. After school, she dialed the number she was given and that sexy, strong voice answered.

"Hi, sweetie. What are you up to?"

"Uh, I don't know. Nothing. What are you up to?" Teresa sounded like the rookie she knew herself to be. She had the house phone cradled close to her face, hiding in the kitchen pantry and feeling seemingly safe from discovery, the mother figure comfortably perched in front of the boob tube in the front room, cocktail clutched. She lowered her register, just in case, and added, "I loved kissing you last night."

"Ooh, nice. I'm finishing up here. Do you still want to have dinner with me?"

"Sure," she was quiet after that, having absolutely nothing to add and figuring she'd let Barbara tell her what to do next. All day she had considered

over and over what she would do once she
was alone with Barbara, but felt like it
all seemed so difficult to achieve. All
this talking nonsense got in the way.

"I'll pick you up at 8:00. Is that good
for you?" Barbara was purring.

"Yes, absolutely." Teresa gave
directions then hung up the phone.
Nerves permeated her every move as she
prepared for the evening, managing to
silence them for a moment when
informing her mother with a detached
cool that she'd be having dinner at a
friend's house, maybe staying the night.
Her mother appeared nonplussed, so she
figured the ruse had worked. She forged
ahead with as much confidence as she
could muster.

Barbara looked hot as fuck in her
fast car and thick, black eyeliner,
rendering Teresa speechless. Barbara
kissed her deeply right in front of the
house she shared with her mother,
leaving Teresa squirming at the thought
of being caught. She only started
breathing normally as they pulled away.
Barbara seemed fine with the discomfort,
as if she knowingly could handle any
resistance because she was in the
business of converting straight girls.
Teresa didn't know what to expect and

that seemed to be the most exciting stance to take in life. Watch and learn. And she was wide-eyed enough and ready to do just that.

Dinner consisted mostly of flirting and groping with minimal conversation. Barbara seemed to know everyone at the joint, which was more of a gay bar than a restaurant, carrying herself with a demeanor that was contagious. This stunning lesbian inspired a side of Teresa that felt more like the Trick of her own fantasies. Movement seemed fluid and laughter came easy. Flirting was suddenly second nature, as if she conducted herself this way all the time. She appreciated the freedom she felt in being so open and daring, and when Barbara suggested they go back to her apartment after picking up the check without missing a beat, there seemed no other play to make. She was heading in the direction of wherever this siren called.

Once inside the stylish apartment, the kissing and the groping began immediately. Teresa liked this kind of attention and responded with her mouth and fingers. It all seemed to be moving so fast, however, coupled with the vodka cranberry cocktails she reluctantly obliged during dinner. She didn't want to seem ungrateful or prudish. Yet that awkward feeling in her stomach triggered a fear she was performing badly. She had to tell herself to keep moving through whatever this was, that she was doing fine.

They moved to the bedroom and Barbara pushed Teresa down onto her big, soft bed, peeling her pants off with dexterity. She took off her own clothes and pushed her mouth onto Teresa's parts, flicking her tongue wildly and humming as her naked body writhed above. It began to take on this forced eroticism, especially when Barbara presented the scenario with a new toy, a huge black dildo she proceeded to strap on and push inside Trick with some real difficulty. They had to keep applying lubricant and there was some moaning, but overall it was awkward since Teresa was nowhere near reaching an orgasm because she couldn't relax through all this performing. It didn't feel like much, just a lot of pressure down below, but it was still a turn on and Teresa went home happy to have experienced something so real, even if it was surreal.

It was no surprise she never saw that woman again. She simply stopped taking her calls. But she never forgot the soft kiss after it was all over, the taste of herself all over the lips of this dynamic woman. Teresa told no one about it and a week after graduation she said her good-bye. The sad look in her mother's eyes produced a brief welling in her own, but she staved off anything foolish like remorse. Her mother had made mistakes, married the wrong man, and that was something she vowed to avoid, marriage. Her tomorrow was wide open. And there was to be no hesitation in her steps. As she climbed the train to take her away from the supposed appeal of suburban routine, she remarked on her own willingness to experience more than most. I am capable of anything, she thought. Whatever it is I'm looking for, let me at it.

It's early evening when James arrives at the loft, pausing to take a deep breath before letting himself in with his own set of keys. Emma is passed out at her computer, head resting in the crook of her arm. He takes one look at her and shakes his head disapprovingly. He begins to undress and heads for the shower. He stops for a moment to consider her, yelling from across the room, "Em! You want to shower before I do?"

She stirs groggily, "No, you go first. I'm going to lie down and take a nap. Wake me in fifteen," she struggles to get up and stumbles into the bed.

James walks to the open kitchen instead and grabs some leftovers from the fridge, popping them into the microwave. "I'm heating something up. You should eat before we go." Emma doesn't respond. James reluctantly places the hot food on the counter and continues to get ready.

After his shower and donning a tuxedo, he stands over the bed, staring at her lifeless body. "Emma! Emma, wake up! It's time to go!"

Emma barely stirs, then returns to her self-induced coma.

"Are you coming? Do you want me to take out your dress? This is important for us! For you!" He begins to shake her. Emma rolls out of bed, falling hard onto the floor. She quickly gathers herself together in a daze and runs to the bathroom. The sound of her vomiting is heard from down the hall. He walks to the bathroom door, annoyed. She pushes past him and falls back into bed. "Great," he said, "And what did I do to deserve this?" He grabs his overcoat and storms out.

The tent houses well-dressed patrons of the arts, the wealth seeping off of their attire and attitudes. The clinking of dishes signals the deft consumption of expensive plates of food, after which mingling is encouraged. James isn't in the mood to cavort with the stuffy elite a moment longer, excusing himself from the table with the glaringly apparent empty seat next to him, and says his half-hearted goodbyes. On his way out, he spots a beautiful woman, although a tad generous with her makeup, by the door. It takes him a moment to recognize her from his brief stint on Wall Street. He remembers always liking her because she could handle herself around men, always up for a good time and savvy enough to excuse herself before things got sloppy. He saddles up to say hello. She laughs light-heartedly at his jokes. He offers up an arm and off they walk, engaged in witty banter. He hails a cab and they climb in together. The cab speeds away.

The sun is slow to come up. James exits a cab in front of Emma's loft. He walks in loudly, not bothering to shut the front door behind him. The loft is dimly lit as he begins undressing out of his tux, throwing it roughly onto the floor, and slides into a pair of jeans and a tee shirt. Emma stirs.

"James?" She lifts her head, dropping it quickly back onto the pillow.

"That's the last event I ever go to alone!" James barks.

"That good, huh?" she replies blearily.

"I want out of this relationship. You're toxic!" he shouts as he begins collecting the things he has kept at her place into a duffle bag.

"Okay," Emma sits up, shaking her head into cognition as she tries to process what is happening.

"Yeah, I didn't expect you'd put up much resistance," he says and walks brusquely towards the door.

"But I started a new book!" she croaks after him. His pace doesn't waver. She watches him walk out, utterly powerless to stop him. He slams the door, as the morning light creeps into the large loft windows, illuminating the moment by magnifying the angles. Her world had stopped making sense long ago; it had become increasingly easier for her to disappear from the harsh criticism found in the world's eyes. Couldn't he see that? Now, she is really alone. She holds her head and whimpers.

She has no choice but to snap out of this fog and get dressed and out the door. The morning's searing light hurts Emma's sensitive eyes as she enters the small church on the Bowery. She spots Teresa immediately, still donning her green army jacket and sweet smile. Emma's half-cracked smile returns the favor. Teresa rushes over to greet her with a warm cup of coffee. They sit at a table and begin talking Emma rubs at her swollen eyes, takes out a yellow legal pad from her messenger bag, and begins asking Teresa questions that quickly become personal. Teresa doesn't seem to mind, answering with an ease that transcends her years. Emma's pen is actively scribbling away, carving one woman's sordid past onto the yellow pages, the hard stuff made easy. Teresa doesn't miss a beat, happy to share. This is a form of release for her and she has the

whimsy of youth on her side. There is no shame in her
game. A sense of peace surrounds both women.

2. In and Out

    The metropolis pops at a tempo that
speaks to the eager heart. There, one
finds the needed push to jumpstart
everything all at once. It is at times
painful, as it constantly flushes out the
phony, terrified, and especially those
who can't take a joke. The city waits for
no one, and as soon as the reality of
that is digested, then one can start
living. There are those that say one year
is nothing in the schema of the concrete
jungle. You are a true native if you can
survive, and thrive, in five. But you must
fight in order to win anything
worthwhile. Otherwise, your appeal falls
short and no one calls because no one
cares, unless you've shown some genuine
interest in their welfare. Then, insofar
as you've injected sufficient partiality,
they'll call to make sure you've read
their book, seen their play, and/or
invested something tangible in their
company. If questions ever come up
concerning the condition of things in
your court, more than likely it is in

relation to their own growth, a look at how well they're doing compared to you. Those questions are posed, more frequently, to make the apathetic feel better about their own ventures. And the answers are very often ignored.

Trick wasn't subscribing. She set it straight within the confines of her genius that she would never be had. To be taken advantage of by anyone would be admitting personal defeat, and the living with that strain was more than she would allow herself to endure. If reality is understood to be that which we make it, she gathered the reigns and marched forward, daring others to keep up, but not counting on it. Therein, she suffered no disappointments and allowed herself many amusements, never at her own expense.

She enrolled in a state school, but her intolerance for imposed discipline put off schooling indefinitely. She sought to make some real money. By twenty-three, she settled into her thoroughly good looks and her inherent propensity to problem solve anything decidedly viable, feeling both carefree girl and astute woman. Short stints at menial jobs in the service industry succeeded only in raising the bar of her standards. The city cost. She was growing restless, relentless without mercy, because she had to have more.

Her apartment, located on the Lower Eastside, she shared with a flight attendant and it seemed to grow smaller by the day. Initially, she didn't care because her roommate was away three weeks out of the month. Trick figured she could entertain without disruption and it was cheap. The neighborhood was sketchy, but she excused most things, deeming her current living conditions as incentive, in her mother's words, to work smarter not harder. You have to start somewhere, she quietly reiterated as she forced herself to ignore the heroin addicts nodding off on the playground benches not a block from her front door. The direction from here was only up.

Her room was unique not in that it faced a courtyard that was shared by the neighboring apartment buildings to the right and back, as many New York City apartments had those, but because to the left was a beautiful synagogue that had been abandoned and was now being utilized for filming music videos and housing events. The trees and flowers someone cared to maintain gave her enough to be happy about when peering

36

out the horrid, metal grating that shielded the windows and protected her from intruders. It took her no time to feel a certain likeness to a caged animal, sending her out to hit the streets more often than maybe she would have preferred. She didn't like to feel trapped.

The workday for many was winding down as hers was being set into motion. This particular Friday she had the place all to herself. Distant noises from the street, a constant for the city no matter where one resided, were strangled by chords and sampled riffs compiling music that had few listeners. The playlist she chose while she dressed, using her absent roommate's stereo, was an electronically synthesized orchestra that had been passed along by an odd boy from her Calculus class taken as a junior in high school. The music turned her nerve endings into firecrackers.

After sitting on the awful blue and white striped loveseat that supported the claim of a "furnished apartment" in the ad, she kicked up a leg and crossed it over the other in the reflection of the full-length mirror she had dragged from the bathroom, now leaning precariously against the wall, whereby she could get a good look at her body in motion. The shoes were given a nod and the black, laced stockings could not have been more perfect. It was the first time she wore such sexy things. They came all the way up to her thigh, and had elasticity at the top that felt sticky on her skin. She slid her legs every which way to test the give and they stayed put. Her blood was moving more quickly than usual as she took in this vision of herself she expected to see since childhood. What little money she had saved from her last job waiting tables at a local French brasserie went towards a mini-shopping spree that would accommodate her first few days on the job. A short, red dress, tight, was the perfect choice. The first expensive item in her possession, it garnered whistles and catcalls from males passing her by on the street. She only cared about the way it felt stretched across her firm breasts. Silk defined pleasure found in material yet again. "Now it begins," she said aloud, laughing to herself.

She positioned herself at the bar and waited. Finding this place had been difficult. The door was unmarked, except for the number 147. There was no storefront to speak of. If you didn't know it was there, you could walk right by it and never know. She was told about this East Village joint by a dancer at a strip club and she wanted to see for herself the availability of its clientele. The dark atmosphere held a lot of potential. At this point anything goes. She finally felt up for this challenge.

The scruffy bartender was her type, if she considered having a type, but not at all her prey. She knew the sad deal. Slinging beers brought in a couple of bills by the end of a long shift and that kind of work, breaking your back for a boss's gain, had sufficiently turned her off. She had fixedly deemed herself worth more, concluding her desired lifestyle was well out of reach in relation to her current pathetic bank account balance and pitiless earnings if she continued as a civil servant. Even if the bartender continued to glance over in her direction, what could he provide her? Dinner and drinks on a Friday night? Of course not, he'd have to work at the bar until closing. Even on an average Wednesday, how far could that take her? It would be a waste of both of their time, as she'd only end up breaking his heart anyway. Leave him be, she thought, bigger and better fish to fry. However, she wasn't about to shut any doors. She entertained the notion of covert operating. This bartender could potentially become her ally. Best to keep him close and see how he could become useful.

The first lone man in assumed a spot at the end of the bar, ordered a drink, and took to her immediately. Trick had perfected her instincts and already acquired a collection of responses to the insatiable male appetite. Her favorite fantasies, though, always resulted in the destruction of another's ego. She couldn't help but dare a battle of wills, which would inevitably lead to her rendering her opponent utterly futile and only then, when the male felt like there was no chance in hell he could ever get with a bitch like her, would she chase him, to his delight. Most belonged in the category "easy mark" and if he played too hard to get, she would simply move on. There were so many others and she wanted no headache. As she saw it, she had work to do to bridge the gap between her fantasies and reality. It was, like most things, a numbers game.

"Bartender," she announced, "I think I'm thirsty!" She met the eyes of the stooge who mired his face with a coy

40

smile, instantly incriminating himself as lacking the imagination to play hard to get. "Do I look thirsty to you?"

"Well, now that you mention it," the boob almost stuttered.

She peeled herself off the barstool and eased her way onto the one to his left, sliding her legs next to his. She felt him stir and nearly rolled her eyes at how little effort it took to get him going. "What are we drinking, Tom?" She reached for his glass and drained the remaining liquid. The whiskey had had enough time to chill, and went down without argument.

"You weren't kidding," he said.

"Don't be so sure. I'm not called Trick for nothing."

She signaled to the bartender for two more. The cute bartender smirked, shaking his head. "Ye given me customer a hard time?" he spoke with a thick Irish accent.

"I think he can handle it," she didn't smile, eyeballing him and pressing a finger up to her lips to silence him from further friction. He made their drinks while holding her gaze. Trick couldn't deny his look evoked something in her, but forced herself to focus on enterprise.

"So, what do you do?" She placed a hand gently on top of the dupe's arm.

"Wall Street."

Perfect, she mouthed, throwing away the next word as if his response was of no consequence. "Married?"

"Are you?" He played that coy smile on his face again but his eyes flickered with concern. The last thing he'd need right now was an entanglement with a kept woman to interrupt his pending status as the next Big Swinging Dick on the floor. He worked hard, but that didn't stop him from playing hard, and there were those that wanted him to suffer. He'd recently considered a higher path, to separate himself from all the bullshit and for all he knew, this could be a set up. Paranoia in his business was necessary.

"Of course not. But who cares, really?" She loved this part. She had thought of pulling it off so many times. With her painted face and dress she thought of herself as a woman of thirty, competing with the sexual peak that was her right as an independent woman on the town. She grew excited with the start. He was cute enough in his dark blue blazer and tie. She took his hand and moved it between her legs, separating her

42

thighs to allow room for exploration, the hairs his fingers found with enthusiastic abandon were soft and damp. Abruptly, he stopped and looked away.

"That's enough," he whispered.

"That too much for you?" she chided. The bartender was eyeballing her again, keeping her in apparent check. She didn't mind it, but the bar was getting more crowded and she needed this deal sealed. If not, she'd have to summon up the courage to find another mark.

"It's just… You're very beautiful. I'm not sure what you want from me."

"Come off it, Tom. You can handle it."

"My name's Jeff. And you're playing a very adult game here."

"Ooh," she cooed. "Serious type. Don't worry, Jeff. This will be over soon, and then you can go back to your exciting life of adding and subtracting numbers. But first, I want to ask you something. Jeff?"

"Yeah?"

"Are you having any fun?"

"If I close this deal I'm working on, everyone I know will have to tell me to stop having so much fun."

"Sounds like you got your head in the game. How about getting some head?"

"What did you say?"

"Don't be so shy. I'm here to help, that's all. You know, clear your mind, ease some tension."

"Are you serious?" he started to chuckle.

"I'm having a blast, you're the one who needs to lighten up. Glad to see you smiling again, though. Thought I lost you there." She began caressing his thigh, turning her body around to face him square. She picked up the fresh drink and sipped. "What turns you on, anyway?"

"What do you mean?" he gave her a sideways glance, taking a drink.

"What do you want to have happen?" she asked the question innocently.

"You're a hooker, aren't you," he dared.

She scoffed. "My time is valuable, if that's what you mean."

"You weren't just being friendly?"

"What girl do you know is that friendly? You're not that naïve, and I certainly didn't approach you with the idea of settling down with a bunch of screaming little kids. Be honest with yourself, it's much easier. What do you say to some fun? You work hard, you deserve it."

"Don't you want more out of life?" He stared into her eyes, causing her nerve to slip a little and forcing her to look away.

"Indeed I do. My life is my own. I certainly didn't approach you for a lecture, Jeff." She held out a hand. "The name's Trick."

"So, sex, then," he said, accepting her hand.

"That's right."

"How much?"

Trick lowered her voice. "A hundred bucks for a blowjob. Three to five for an hour, depending on what goes." She sat up straight and rocked side to side on the stool, the thin silk sticking to her.

He looked around to see if the other patrons could read the situation and that made her laugh out loud. People were so wrapped up in their own bullshit that they couldn't care less and this made her like the place that much more. She could sense he was nervous, so she made a move. "You got a car?"

"My truck's parked out front."

"Let's go."

"Where?"

"To your truck! What's the matter with you?" She hopped off the barstool, grabbing his hand and her short, black, leather jacket. She met resistance in his grasp. She jumped the gun, maybe. But he downed his drink and threw some money on the bar with his free hand, incidentally tipping the bartender sixteen bucks. The bartender's eyes followed Trick out.

Once inside his truck, she was struck by the new car smell. "Nice," she said and was quieted when the proximity to this complete stranger in an enclosed space was actualized. He put the truck in drive, and they rode like two awkward teenagers on their way to Lookout Point to grope and make out. He finally broke the silence by turning on some music, something by Phil Collins. She rolled her eyes and stared out the window and wondered what the hell she was doing here. Then, just as quickly, her insecurity was replaced by the excitement of the kill. She was going to do this!

They pulled up to a block in Soho and he parked the truck. They stared forward. She turned to him and smiled. He smiled back.

"Let's make this nice." She started to open the door.

He stopped her by grabbing hold of her wrist. "I've never done this before," he said, his eyes boring holes in her skull.

46

Trick took a deep breath. "Like I said…"

"No, really."

"It's okay, Baby. I'm going to take care of you. It'll be fun. Please don't worry."

"Can you not talk to me like that?"

"Like what?"

"Like you would any… I don't want to feel like a stranger."

"It's okay, Jeff. We're going to have a good time. No big deal." She wondered again, what was she doing? But she kept her wits about her, leaning over to gently kiss his tight lips, running her hands through his thick hair. I can do this, she thought. If only he knew it was my first time, too. But then, a Wall Street guy who's never been with a hooker? How truthful was he being with her? She withheld judgments and used her fantasy to her advantage. Best to play the part. She had to get through this, after all, to prove to herself, at the very least, that she could do it. She wasn't even sure what she would let him do for five hundred bucks, but knew that he'd be good for at least the three she'd proposed.

"Is this your place?" she said as she pulled away from the kiss that was not so terrible after all. At least he smelled nice.

"Yeah."

"Do you have any liquor?"

He smiled at the question, and opened his car door. Relieved, she followed.

Upstairs, the loft he called home took her breath away. It was a raw, open space, tastefully furnished. He lived alone and obviously did very well for himself. He tossed his keys into a bowl by the front door, shed his blazer, and walked over to a full bar built into the open kitchen. He poured them some whiskey and put on music using a remote control that he pointed in the general direction of the far wall. She searched but couldn't find the source of the trancelike music, but took pleasure in being served by him. He walked her over to the white, leather couch and they sat and sipped. He made the first move, grabbing her head and pushing it towards his dick. She stopped him, surprised.

"Whoa, boy," she wasn't sure what he thought he was doing.

"What, isn't that what you said?"

"You have to tell me what you want first," she said.

"You said head, right?"

48

"Yeah, but you have to pay me first. And, you know, if you want more."

"I think you're hot," he said through a big, toothy grin.

"Thank you."

"Take your dress off," he said and put down his drink on the mahogany coffee table.

"Can you please tell me what you think you'll want?"

"I want to see what I'm paying for."

She stood and took a breath and said, "Look, wise guy. This can be easy if you make it that way. And who knows? Maybe I'll come back whenever you want. You're a good-looking guy and I liked kissing you. Don't make me regret coming here." She hoped her voice didn't betray the fear that was rising in the pit of her stomach. "Make this worthwhile for yourself. I'm here for your pleasure."

He smiled. "Okay, Trick. You're right. Sorry."

"Do you want to fuck me, Jeff?"

"Yes."

"Do you have three hundred bucks?"

He took out his wallet and pulled out three bills and laid them on the table. She folded them and tucked them in her jacket pocket. She looked around for the bedroom, and couldn't find it. "Here?"

she asked, indicating the couch. He shook his head and led the way to the bed that was hidden under curtains in the far corner of the big room. He took off her dress, she stripped him of his work attire, and they fucked and it was fine. In fact, he gave her two hundred more for another round of consummation.

Trick hit the streets, feeling proud of her success. She knew she could do it! Five hundred bucks for an hour's worth of "work". It was ingenious! She decided she deserved a drink. There was a little bar down the street from where Jeff lived. Soho was such a nice part of town, and because it was a beautiful spring night, going home didn't appeal to her at all. She had a pocket full of money, and the thought crossed her mind that she was inherently good at this. A second glance revealed that the bar was connected to a swanky hotel, confirming her natural instincts. She straightened her posture to refresh her attitude.

Heads turned upon her entrance. That's right, she thought, look. She smiled, and took her time walking through the bar. She was enjoying herself, taking in the décor and relishing in it without apology. Eyes stayed with her. They liked her flavor.
50

The men served up interest, then waited to see what she'd do. They were corporate types well on their way to getting drunk, by the sounds of it. Trick took a seat at a table in the corner. When the waitress came over, she ordered a whiskey, neat. Looking back at the suits, she settled on the one guy who refused to look away. He appeared well home-fed. She stared back, offering a raised eyebrow delivered with the tilt of her head. He took the cue and approached, his pint of beer in hand.

"You alone?" he spoke gently.

"Not anymore, I think," she kicked out the chair across from her. He peered back at his group of friends and then sat heavily, making the chair sigh.

"What brings you here?" she guessed he was a guest of the hotel and was right.

"We're opening up a new office. I'm from Lincoln, Nebraska, far cry from New York, I tell ya. But man, I've always loved this city."

"Best city in the world," she proclaimed with glee. Nebraska! The waitress came back and set her whiskey down in front of her. She reached into her jacket pocket and he stopped her.

"Please, let me. Put it on my tab, will you?" The waitress gave a quick smile,

and walked off. "What about you? How did
you end up here?"

"I always knew I would. Something
about the electricity of this many people
in one place. So much opportunity."

"What do you do?" He grinned
sheepishly.

"I know one thing I'd like to do. Take
you to your room and fuck your brains
out."

He sat back, "Whoa."

"What's wrong with that?" She downed
half the glass with a wink.

"Didn't get your name, little lady," he
looked around nervously to the
neighboring tables to see if anyone was
listening. He thought he saw the couple
next to them smirking and grew
uncomfortable.

"Didn't ask for yours, either. I don't
give a shit. The less I know the better.
You don't even live here, officially. And I
don't need a boyfriend. I'm horny as hell."

"That's rich," he laughed nervously,
grabbing at his necktie.

"I happen to be very good. The last
guy was pleased. I left him with a stupid
smile on his face," she said smiling,
enjoying the feeling of being in charge.

"The last guy, huh?"

"Yes. I could do the same for you. You got a couple hundred bucks?" She played her tongue on her top lip, amused at his squirming. "It can be so easy and a lot of fun."

"For you, maybe. I'm married. I came over because I hate to see a woman sitting alone, that's it." He got up to leave. She got up and moved in step with him to the bar. The other men turned to see them approach.

"Hey Jim, who's your friend? She's cute!" The guys put forth friendly demeanors. Jim's face was strained. "You feeling okay, Jim?"

"I'm tired is all. Long day," he exhaled loudly as he signed for the drinks, while Trick stood deciding what to do next. Something had gone terribly wrong. Where was her head? He turned to say goodnight, giving her a quick, gentlemanly salute. She watched him walk away, thought twice and quickly followed him further into the hotel's lush interior. She met up with him waiting for the elevator.

"I'm sorry, I didn't mean to turn you off. The point was actually the opposite," she pushed her hair behind her ears, and implored him with a look. It wasn't that she didn't care, she did. These were the beginning stages of her career as a "working girl". She didn't like to fail and she wanted to know why he had balked. "Are you not attracted to me?"

"It's not… Don't be silly. You're a beautiful girl." In the lights of the lobby, she saw he was much older than she originally perceived, old enough to be her father, maybe. He watched for the coming elevator, wringing his hands.

"You've never cheated on your wife?" She sounded more amazed than she meant to. Leave him alone, she thought, but couldn't move. Her legs were locked. What was she trying to prove? Years of fruitless pining for affection from anyone remotely resembling a father figure resulted in a sense of entitlement to treat others as she liked, hardly taking any heed as to the way she could make others feel. Now, this strange, sad man held her attention, as if the very virtues of integrity and honor were embodied in his saggy being, as if he alone could provide respite from the things she didn't understand, with the power to hurt her if he denied her that refuge.

The ding sounded the elevator's arrival and action needed to ensue either way. "I… Do you want to come up?"

He offered. Trick wanted to make him as happy as when she first saw him moments ago, strutting his stuff in the big city, brave enough to approach a woman like her. She stepped into the elevator.

The door was heavy. She pushed hard and as she leaned her weight into it, the wind rushed her face and she was happy for it. Finding a cab would be the only thing that could bring forth the comfort she desperately needed, shelter from the storm. However, the empty cobblestone streets paraded no such offering. She'd have to walk to the nearest avenue. Her legs scraped against one another as she shuffled. She pinched her jacket at the neck and preceded, head down. It wasn't until she heard sound approaching that she raised her face and looked up and out at the world, to find another woman, older and more sensible, walking by. Short, cropped hair and a clean face topped off the flat squish of rubber shoes and wide backside hidden by a black, formless dress. It was in that moment of quiet acknowledgement, an unspoken gesture that admits to the other of the moment shared so briefly by two complete strangers on the streets of a big city, that this homely woman thought it better not to present a warmer version of hello, how are you, but instead indulged herself in a look of disgust and scowled. It caught Trick off guard. There was a misstep in her heels and a quick recovery, but the incident did not go unnoticed as the burn traveled up to the tip of her ears.

There was a considerable amount of tax she paid for her easy money. She strangled this new truth as it placed strain on her ankles and chipped its way at her peace of mind. That scowl sent her head straying when she needed most to focus on the road underfoot. She was instantly tried, but asked for no judgment, denounced without advocate by those who spent their evenings feeling safe from discomfort or fear of threat. Her prosecutor's stance was a situation rough for the wear, not hers, as she peered out of shadowed eyes to navigate her way home. The misconceiver thought she the only keeper of happiness and health when the rot of a marriage and the resistance of the spoiled wifey to spread 'em due to a non-existence sex drive sent the man out in the first place seeking solace. This hypocrisy belies professional gals their reason to boast because it is in this condemnation these

56

brave girls, who have grown into women warriors, find their full voice, laugh out loud and often, dress as outrageous birds, feel the most alive, and at their very best remain untouchable.

Jim hadn't been a sweet family man. He surrendered to her seduction immediately by pushing her down and sodomizing her. Jim landed a few soft blows with his fist to the back of her head. He beat her, making gruff sounds as he entered her, then sobbed. Trick squeezed her eyes shut. It grew quiet inside her head, and she was surprised that she was experiencing something like pleasure. He was passionate and wild, and fell out of her when it was all over, gasping. He took a long while to compose himself. She waited, curled up next to him and began to giggle and for the life of him, he thought he'd never understand it. Something must be wrong with her, he deducted. But he did feel better, the rage of a lifetime of rejection released in his orgasm. She was the only woman who had ever let him enter her ass. It had been retired as an option, declaring the same woman his lover for the last seventeen years. He would stay married, deciding that this would remain a carnal secret he'd hold close to his chest with ungodly satisfaction. If anything, he could visit the experience in his fantasies, when his hand was full of the flesh that grew between his legs. As he drifted off to sleep, he had thoughts of home and his kind wife. He felt sure he'd stay put in the suburbs of Lincoln. Somehow, he figured, this demon inside of him had been silenced.

Chapter 3

James sits at his desk in his corner office of a Midtown high rise, overlooking surrounding skyscrapers. He punches the speakerphone button and dials Emma's cell phone. He clutches Emma's first two chapters tightly in his hands as the phone rings. There are red-inked notes written all over the top page. He grabs at the neck of his shirt and takes a deep breath.

Emma stirs at the sound of the phone's incessant ringing. She fumbles to grab it from the nightstand, dropping it to the floor and cursing. She peers at the screen and sees who is calling through half slitted eyes. She places the device near her head, returning her tired eyes to the closed position. "Good morning," her voice cracks slightly.

"Hello, Emma. Do you have time to go over your work with me right now? How's your head?"

"Good. Glad to know you still care," she clears her throat.

"Don't be like that. You always know where to find me."

"You used to call every day. You are still my agent, after all, even if you gave up on us."

"I didn't call for this, Em. I'm very busy. I have a lot of new writers to deal with."

"Well, your secretary Suzy hates me."

"She doesn't hate anybody. Don't be ridiculous," James stands and begins to pace.

"Fine, let's hear it. Put me out of misery."

"Stop it. It's not that bad. But I need more. Something to believe in. A human element. You want your readers to like her, right? That's what your fans are expecting. Give us something to care about. Right now she's coming across as a sociopath."

"Wow, you really read it," she laughs. "Cut her a break. She's still exploring. She's taking risks, yes, but on her own terms."

"Alright, but the tragedy of her situation reads as self-induced, therefore it's difficult to be empathetic. Her career choice is not enviable."

"Oldest profession in the book. Don't judge her character on curb appeal."

"But most people won't identify with it right off the bat. No empathy, and you won't grab your reader's attention."

"Jesus, James, she's not walking the streets at Hunt's Point with a needle full of heroin dangling from her arm. Not yet, anyway. She's about to go on a journey, and it's not always going to be pretty. Right now she's young and exploring. She's pushing the envelope to see what unfolds. A brave character with an unenviable career choice, by society's standards. But she chooses to work for herself and she's decidedly enjoying it."

"What else is there?" he chuckles.

"Exactly."

"Well, shit. Maybe that's why you're still in bed and I'm sitting here breathing in corporate AC all day."

"C'mon, you look great under fluorescent lighting."

"Smell my finger."

"You still using the middle one?"

James smiles, "It means so much to me that you remembered."

"It wasn't that long ago," she replies sadly.

James quickly changes the subject. "Wanna hear some juice that Suzy spilled at the water cooler the other day? Husband Frank has been too tired to fuck her for nine months. She says they may be setting a new personal record for married couples. So he comes home drunk the other night and he lies down on the couch to watch some television. She's lying there in bed waiting for him and when she hears the TV go on she decides to piss on his side of the bed."

"Wow, that redefines sleeping in the wet spot."

"Tell me, Em, what position would a woman do that from? You think she squatted?"

"My guess is she did it lying down."

"How lazy does a guy have to be not fuck his wife for nine months?"

"Maybe she ought to piss on Frank. He might like it."

Suzy's voice comes through on the intercom. "James, Tom from Harper Collins is on line four. And don't forget your lunch appointment with Charles today at twelve-thirty."

"Thank you, Suzy."

Suzy adds, "and please say hi to Emma for me."

"Will do," James pushes the button, hanging up on Suzy. "See, Em? Suzy doesn't hate you. She told me to say hi."

"His climbing back into bed, finding it full of piss. Such a great visual."

"Maybe you can write it in somewhere."

"I'll be sure to file it."

James addresses a staff member who walks by his office. "Put those over there. Let Jonathan know we have that conference call with Sam in ten minutes. Sorry, Em. How about dinner a week from Friday?"

"What's that about?"

"There's interest in the film rights to Neil's last book. Listen, I can meet you at nine for dinner next Friday. Raoul's?"

She props herself up. "That sounds fine," she says.

"Ok, gotta get back to work. Make me proud."

"Oh Captain, my Captain."

"Call me when you have the next chapters," James hangs up, leaving Emma in silence, minus the distant sounds of twenty-four seven New York City traffic permeating her walls. She groans and lies back down, pulling a pillow over her head.

Emma sits at her desk, staring at the screen of her laptop. Her cigarette needs to be ashed but she doesn't seem to notice. She stares into nothingness.

It's happy hour at a local East Village watering hole. A nearby table is filled with young patrons boisterously trying to top one another, shouting over each other to be heard. Emma sits at the bar and listens, writing on her yellow legal pad. She orders another drink, then leans in to eavesdrop on their conversation. A few one-liners make her laugh and she's sure to take note. She feels a part of them, encompassed by their carefree energy. Tomorrow may never come and they seem fine with that. For a moment, Emma imagines a life without worry, as if this one moment could be extended for the duration of her entire life if she could only remember how good it feels to live presently and without fear. She smiles at these kids not much younger than her but seemingly much younger and quietly thanks them for reminding her to stop taking this shit so seriously.

The evening brings with it a rare cool breeze. Emma and Teresa get out of a cab in front of a seedy strip joint. One of the two bouncers sees Teresa and gives her a gigantic bear hug, lifting her up off the sidewalk. "Been a long time, pretty girl," the bouncer says.

"Been out of the game for a while. Thanks for noticing," Teresa smiles.

"Good for you. Gone, but not forgotten." He personally escorts them to the back stage dressing room. Girls are adjusting their lingerie and applying makeup into wall mirrors. Teresa introduces Emma to a thin blonde, visibly drunk and high on something, in a black thong, garter belt, and a lacy black bra. They find a corner to sit and talk. As the blonde responds to Emma's questions with reckless abandon, Emma scribbles voraciously on her yellow pad.

"Oh, I have to use before I work. It's the only way I can get on that stage. We girls call this liquid courage!" she smiles, raising a glass filled with iced vodka to her lips. "Cheers!"

Emma returns the smile, sympathetically.

64

Emma is back in her loft, quickly typing away at her desk, cigarette dangling from her mouth. She stops to turn to her notes on her yellow pad, finds what she is looking for, and continues to type, a determined expression blanketing her face.

3. Checking In

With the warm weather, spirits soared. There were nights the city seemed to call everyone out of their rented boxes, on missions to discover the inner workings of one clever head to another, with big plans to make one's lot in life even bigger. Recognizing agendas didn't take away from the adventure of finding a new way to attack a project with a prospective partner, and one was measured on the daring to get the job done. One out of ten, a guy had a genuinely authentic thought. In a case like that, he'd require confirmation that this was the next best thing, necessarily throwing caution to the wind, needing not to protect his bright idea, but to rally others to help him see it to the end and set the world on fire. A bright idea is a valuable commodity, but starting at the bottom with little to no resources was harder than the pavement you had to pound on to get said idea accomplished.

All this talk of creative ingenuity made Trick think: What am I giving back? It was obvious, answering her own question. Making someone feel good and sexy and desired was more than most cared to offer a society seeking instant self-gratification. But after an evening spent with her gregarious girlfriend Pam, a film producer she met at a bar a few months back with steely determination and even quicker wit, and a couple of blowhards from an advertising agency with entrepreneurial slants, she pondered what a life centered on giving back to the world at large would be like, something to be remembered by. Of course she wanted to make a difference. To slag on that duty, as a humanitarian at heart, would be careless and stupid. Life was so glorious and held infinite potential, so much so it sometimes made her head spin. She was growing more pleased with herself every day. What bothered her, though, was the leaving of something behind that most of these upstarts she ran into talked about. They continued to refer to it as "making

66

a mark" and it challenged her ambitions. At first, her coy answers to such inquiries brought jeers and laughter. "What's wrong with that? I want to make sure every human has clean drinking water. We've become far too selfish as a society," she heard herself say and remembered a time not so long ago when putting herself first was the only thing she knew to do, had to do, in order to survive the pain of being left by her deadbeat Dad. She still held fast to her philosophy that she needed no man to achieve greatness. A lot good it did her mother, sitting at home every night in pieces over the lost love of a man. Her Mom was a great lady any man would be proud to call home and still, it hadn't been enough. Perhaps it wasn't in the striving for being the great woman behind a great man, but instead being a great woman on her own accord. And that meant exacting positive change for the world at large. A tall order for a Tuesday night in the big city, her cohorts made sure to tell her that, but it didn't shake her resolve. Life was hard enough without dreaming. She found being hopeful for humanity a far better cry than standing on the mountaintop, judging the lot of them. And at this hour, fueling her drinking buddies with something resembling hope was the best medicine to administer to soothe the failings of the temporarily downtrodden, even if she had no solid game plan for pulling anything off at present. The glory is found in the striving, even if they try to take the piss out of you by laughing at your bravado. But she never blamed them, wasted no time growing cross, and never worried for them because they were young and optimistic enough on their own to see light at the end of their impoverished tunnel. The city held promise for better, the very reason they migrated there in the first place.

As she thoroughly enjoyed her freedom from real responsibility, she cherished the idea that there was something out there that was bigger than her. She felt it most when she laid her head down to get a few hours rest before rising early on a sleeping city, her favorite time of the day. The mornings held wonder for her, especially Sundays. She'd joke to herself that the city that never sleeps was as peaceful as any suburb as she walked the empty streets and contemplated having some sort of game plan. It is here for the taking, she thought, if only I knew what that thing worth wrestling to the ground was. She sent her breath to the bottom of her belly and let it out slowly. In time, girl, all will be revealed. Keep at it and don't let anyone shake your resolve. No matter what you decide on, it will be good because it's all yours to make. No one will take you away from you because you're all you've got and you damn well won't let them.

She bought a newspaper and sat down to a hardy breakfast and a bottomless cup of coffee. She liked what caffeine did to enliven her nerves, putting them en guarde. After flipping through most of the headlined articles, she pushed the paper aside and looked around the café. There were few professionals in this neighborhood, mostly tortured freelance artists, or young mothers up early with their curious babies. She wondered if the guy she saw walking his terrier in jogging attire and sneakers and smoking a cigarette had, in fact, plans to go for a jog at all. She figured he'd just go back to sleep after the dog had his morning piss. Trick felt a little tired herself, signaling for another cup of coffee. The owner of the joint came over, a barrel-chested man in his forties, sporting a salt and peppered beard and a

full head of tussled hair. His smile
warmed her.

"How is everything?" he poured her
another full cup.

"I love this place. Home away from
home," she smiled.

"I'm Gary. This is my place."

"I figured," she said. "I always see
you here."

"Have you been to my other
restaurant? We opened around the corner.
Baby Gary's, named after my son. He's Gary,
too." He removed her breakfast dishes
from the table and headed back to the
kitchen.

"Thanks! I'll check it out!" she called
to his back. She couldn't decide what to
do next. She had nothing planned for the
day and needed desperately to feel a
sense of accomplishment. She hadn't
worked in over a week, last entertaining
a party of three, a couple she had met
prior and their hapless friend, out for
dinner and drinks. She was hired to take
the friend home with her and was
supposed to show him a good time, without
his knowledge she was a "working girl".
The couple had paid her in advance
because they felt sorry for him and had
specifically asked for absolute
discretion over the business deal. "Take

70

care of him. It's been a while," they had told her. But after bringing him back to her place, he had only wanted a blowjob. The rest of the time he wouldn't stop going on about the last girl that left him and how broken hearted he was. The evening was too depressing a thought to revisit. She knew it was strange to feel this way, but her feelings had been mildly hurt when he had denied indulging in her pussy. Not that it was anybody's loss. But it had made her feel almost unwanted, like she wasn't able to give it away even after it was already paid for. Rejection can arrive in the most unusual forms. Yet, she had to force herself to refuse anything that placed doubt on the value of her goods. As a commodity, she figured she was worth every dollar. She simply called it a night after pleasuring him orally then enduring his sob story. She had to give herself extra credit for being a good listener in the presence of such heartache. Sometimes guys just need someone to talk to. Nothing wrong with that.

She paid her bill, stood, and stretched the morning funk out of her system. Joining a gym had crossed her mind but was replaced by another thought immediately, that of shopping, thus rendering the attempt at physical fitness silly because she lacked the dedication to work out. It was an easy discipline to put off because the constancy of that lifestyle she found annoying. She was already in great shape. Maybe later, she decided, when I need it.

Outside, the sun hit her face and she turned towards home, remembering that her roommate Daisy would be returning today from her stint in Greece and she wanted to avoid hearing the mundane escapades of a woman newly committed to David, an ex-Marine Corps sniper with tattoos on every visible body part except the face, yet still game for the adventures that traveling to foreign lands brought her. Her stories were wrought with averted guilty pleasures, and they sent Trick cringing. Daisy knew she shouldn't indulge, and wouldn't, even if her man was thousands of miles away. Her stories had set-up but no follow through. What the conscience propagated was still a mystery for Trick. She was her own master, thank you very much, and even Daisy's delicate constitution couldn't convince her that it was better to maintain something pseudo special and remotely dependable. Anything resembling commitment reeked. No chance, no fucking chance. It bored her to think of it. Answering to one man? Why? Was Daisy that shortsighted that she needed someone else calling her shots? There was no question her jaunts to exotic places held the magic of the chase. It seemed stupid to pretend that the guy waiting at home would be worth missing out on the delicious opportunity to taste dick of a different land. Trick imagined the cultured dick, the color and the smell. Rich suggestion of spices permeating pores, coupled with unique perceptions of the world they originated from. She simply could not wait to travel.

The next thought was of her mother. It was too early for any of the stores she liked to frequent to be open, so she started walking towards the nearest park and wondered how her mother was fairing. Only a two-hour train ride away, they hadn't talked in months. Occasionally, she'd hear a message from home confirming love and certain missing, albeit through slurred speech, but Trick pushed any possibility for a visit out of her mind because she needed to get a few things going first so that her reporting back wouldn't result in more questions than answers. Trick understood that her ruse needed an airtight presentation. Where did her money come from? How was she getting by? All the mother figure needed to know to feel comfort was that she had many things lined up and she'd eventually be fully employed and in turn would make a wonderful life for herself. I make myself proud, Mama, and that should be enough for anyone who wants to know how I'm doing. Still, the diversion didn't exclude a sense of loss. She missed her mother now more than ever, and the down time between jobs left her feeling vulnerable. At times like these, she supplanted the solitude with a game of chess.

The men that played chess in Washington Square Park were serious about one thing, at least. Their filthy appearances visibly clashed with their acquired skill at beating the pants off anyone who dared to play them, and each and every one of them took their self-proclaimed role as a chess master seriously. It had quickly become one of the more pleasurable impressions she liked to make, sauntering up to the stone tables, looking gullible and oblivious, as if the game held too much mental investment for a pretty girl's

74

sensitivity to appreciate. But they grew to know her modus operandi, and would hoot and holler when they saw her sly approach, a warm welcome that indeed made her feel at home amongst the homeless. They liked the way she looked, smiles spreading over their cracked faces. They shared a mutual affection for each other.

She maintained a healthy memory of an uncle teaching her the game at seven years old. As far as she knew, her uncle was no ordinary man, but then, the family could never elaborate on what he did exactly. There were inferences that her mother's brother worked for the government, or the CIA even, and his constant travel to destinations unknown seemed to somehow confirm it in an exciting way. He was a quiet, beautiful man with very sad eyes and she was always left feeling lonely after his visits because he was like a surrogate father to her. Having children of his own, she sensed that he carried an overwhelming regret over the suffering of his family for his duties. When he came to visit, he was never at liberty to answer her questions, and she had a hundred of them. But he did sit with her and teach her the game until she beat him at it. She hadn't seen him in more years than she could count after that. But the gift he gave her kept on giving.

Trick spotted a younger, black man who beamed in her direction an invitation. He looked like he had showered recently, if he was in fact officially homeless, and she took the available seat opposite him.

"Alright, alright!" he looked around, feeling like the chosen one, and fingered his pieces, tidying the already perfectly aligned formation. "How are you today, little lady?"

"Good morning to you," she smiled politely, deciding on her first move after he engaged a pawn. The chorus of jeers erupting from a nearby game placed her inside that protective bubble; the only thing that mattered when she played the game was the game itself. It made her anxious to claim a win, but always careful to see him take the first round. It insured at the start his dignity. She sought to instill a sense of worth in these men and it never failed to excite the deeply rooted need, existing in all of us, to be loved. This first game was not a battle of skill for her, essentially, but a relinquishing of ego for another's gain.

76

"Don't miss it. Keep your eyes on it," he punched the clock.

She made her next move, one that he expected and closed her eyes, feeling happier than she had in a long time.

"Come on now, don't give it away," his voice sounded off a minor alarm.

She didn't want her slip showing. She tightened the leash a bit. Her next few moves had him running, but in the end he got her.

"There it is." He looked up at her with a gorgeous smile that made her giddy. Success, she thought, smiling back. He was quick to ask, "Wanna go again?"

They always want another when they win. If you beat them outright, more often than not they turn into sour grapes. No man liked being beat by a girl. "Sure," she collected her pieces and set them up. While he was busy with his troops, she discreetly slipped a dollar across the table. He was equally as prudent with the house rules of the park, moving the dollar deftly into his pocket in one continuous motion, the other hand diligent with the handling of his queen.

This time, there was no premeditated mercy. And he loved being taken down quickly by this young woman, clamoring to the others in admiration. "That's the way. Good. Good," as if he were directly responsible for her progress. But when he started preparing for another, she declined, suggesting they keep it even. Save it for a next time. She concluded that having something to look forward to in life was what it was all about. She thanked him as he handed back the same dollar, giggling. He wanted to kiss her, rising from his stone seat and moving closer to where she stood. Refraining from being too swept away in the glory of the moment, Trick walked off, sure of everything at once.

The remainder of the morning had an open, airy quality to it, an assurance that it took very little to make one happy. If you hold your head high and your eyes wide, there were many things to see and so many others to make happier in perhaps inconsequential ways. Complimenting a storeowner on his choice of merchandise, and his due pride in return, was pure pleasure for her. She bought only a few items unique to her newfound personal philosophy towards material items with staying power. Clothes for life. A smooth, stretchy, dark caramel dress that moved with her body, hugging her shoulders and caressing her bare stomach as she walked around the
78

store, the sales girl squealing, to be paired with high-heeled knee-high boots and feathered, dangly earrings, juxtaposing a tough, yet deeply feminine prowl on the town. She was cultivating her own sense of style and that gave her comfort. It was as if something clicked inside of her. And if ever there had been something to worry about, finances or future, it was eclipsed by the goodness of simply being. She liked the way it felt to be sure and held onto it as long as possible, because it was about that time to start drinking and as good as she felt right now, she still had no one to drink with. It was a carefree Sunday and certainly not a day to think about work. In fact, the very thought nearly exhausted her sails. But to go home, change clothes and drop off her new purchases would mean a possible confrontation with Daisy. She didn't want her good mood interrupted by that. Her friend Pam was out of town visiting her family like a good daughter. After perusing the names stored in her cell phone, a thought occurred to her: I need new friends.

She decided on the East Village joint she had met her first client because she suspected the bartender would be there and she was up for a little harmless flirting. He was cute, after all. She was a little underdressed from the last time he saw her, now in the jeans and tank top she threw on this morning, but she could slip into one of her newly purchased tops and that would be fine for a beer or two. It had already been a beautiful morning. Everything else from this point on was gravy.

The place was as she remembered it, secluded and cozy. She walked in with her shopping bags and made a beeline for the restroom. Once inside, she tore the tag off a cream-colored, low-cut silk blouse and slid it over her naked upper torso. She peered at her reflection, happy for her youth and beauty. She felt like a savage inside, wanting so many things out of life, and at the same time becoming her own strong woman. Her small, firm tits would never fall, her face attractive because it was one that inherited sharp cheekbones and a high forehead that indicated openness, inviting others to engage. Her lips were full and hardy, and her nose was the right size and shape to perfectly compliment her face. She was thrilled to have bright green eyes, went as far as secretly discriminating others for not having that good fortune.

She wound up in the very seat she had chosen that first night of her humble beginnings and caught the attention of that cutie pie behind the bar. He saw her and immediately stood his ground, looking at her skeptically.

She said simply, "Hello. I'd like a drink please."

He didn't move from his stance and stared her down. It annoyed her. Who did he think he was? She gave him about six seconds, then began collecting the bags at her feet and headed for the door.

"Whaddya want?" His Irish accent echoed through the sparse bar, still early for drinking but would fill soon enough. She turned to catch his smile fade into an affront, and it was reason enough to rethink this encounter. She didn't need the aggravation, but she did have an intention for returning, right? Now, this sticky feeling she had in her gut while standing in that entranceway, precariously balancing her shopping bags, had her wondering. She became suddenly self-conscious of the condition of her messy hair falling in her eyes. So what, she thought. I can take anything he's serving up and returned to her seat. Who is he to judge me?

"Give me a Stella," she situated her bags underneath her. She suddenly hated how dingy she felt, having skipped a shower that morning. She'd read in a magazine that it was better for your hair not to wash it every day. Now, she regretted that choice.

"Right. Sure. A beer," his tone was still challenging.

"What's that supposed to mean?" she wasn't sure why she felt the need to defend herself.

"Nothin'. A beer sounds tasty right 'bout now."

"Oh, well. Too bad you have to work." She took the pint he set before her in one hand and took a large gulp.

He kept his distance from her, forcing himself to take his time wiping down bottles until he had manhandled them long enough and moved in, standing in front of her position at the bar but avoiding her eyes.

She grew tired of his charade. "What's your deal?"

"What d'ya mean?" he feigned innocence.

"Nothing. You're just standing there."

"I'm workin'," he declared.

82

"No shit," she didn't know what to say next. She was feeling uncomfortable in his presence. "What's up with you?"

"Nothin', what's up with you?"

"Okay… whatever," she turned away from him, feeling sorry for his position in life, for that dumb expression on his face, for maybe her own ineptitude at reaching him in some friendly fashion. She searched for words that never came.

He threw down the dishrag he'd been holding onto and said, "Whadda ye think ye got that I haven't got?"

Oh brother, she thought. Trick instantly wished she were anywhere else but here. The last thing she needed was a guilt trip from some milquetoast who resented her for no apparent reason, and the growing feeling she was having for him reminded her that her least favorite emotion next to jealousy was pity. She clearly made a mistake coming here. She stood, grabbing those cursed bags one last time.

"Wait. Sorry. Don't go," he looked at her with his big green eyes, soft and earnest.

"Who the fuck do you think you are, exactly?" she spit the words out, against her own better judgment to refrain from jumping too quickly to hostility.

"Yer boyfriend." He stated, matter-of-factly.

She was too thrown to even speak. It was the most ridiculous, unexpected thing this day could have delivered. And with that, she stormed out.

There's a period of uncertainty brought on when someone entertains accepting you romantically that leaves you helpless to convince yourself you are due to have something special happen in your life, especially if you're not ready to believe and receive it. Thoughtless pining abounds. Will they change their mind about me once they get to know the real me? Inevitably, an inadvertent resolve takes hold that what they're feeling, surely a momentary lapse of sensibility, will soon be shrouded by the peeled layers of perception that you, as this object of initial affection, are not at all anybody's dream come true, thus rendering their newfound desire anorexic. Further, for the sake of their happiness, you necessitate that their love's magnitude must be redirected towards someone else more deserving of them. Your need to spare them your truth saves you the unwanted exposure of being only that which you are, nothing

84

lovely to hold dear. Self-deprecation can be a bitch when you feel you have nothing worthy to offer.

Trick ran most of the way home. The sun was hours away from delivering its nightly cloak. She hated the disappearance of the light each day and at present had no idea how to fill the rest of it. As she scaled the stairs to her apartment two at a time, she tried to understand what was wrong with her. Why did the thought of having a boyfriend upset her so much? Her stomach was turning as she fought with the key and as she pushed her way through the living area, that churning stomach of hers sank. Her roommate was sitting on the couch watching the blasted boob tube, her brute of a boyfriend helping himself to a beer in the kitchen.

Daisy looked up in surprise. "Hey Teresa! What's up?"

"Hi Daisy," she made her way to her bedroom and threw the packages everywhere, wanting immediately to not be here either. It only now occurred to her she had no place to call home. "Fuck," she spat out and began collecting products for a shower. Her roommate had taken to using them if she kept them in the bathroom. That eluded Trick, as any attempt at drawing boundaries only resulted in an argument about all the things in the apartment that were Daisy's that she had made available to her, like that cursed cable television that Trick had forgotten was even there, or that horrid seersucker couch that added nothing of style to any room. In Daisy's mind they were sisters and, of course, they should share everything. Trick had dropped her case because talking to Daisy was like filling out your medical history in a doctor's office waiting room, or watching paint dry. She absolutely loathed being here and had to get her own place, knowing she had only herself to blame as the day's expenditure spread itself all over her sparse bedroom floor. Her lack of ability to save money disgusted her at present.

She sat on her basic mattress of a bed situated on the floor of her room and tried her hand at composure. From the next room she could hear over the sounds of syndicated sitcom hell what sounded like a fight between Daisy and that new diehard boyfriend of hers, David. Voices dimmed as she tried to make out what the fight-of-the-week was about. Faintly, she heard, "David, please. That's not what happened. David, stop!" and she decided that even a simple shower was going to be too much for her to accomplish under these conditions. She picked up her purse and found a hair tie to pull back the greasy strands. She changed into a sexier pair of boots that elevated her mood, only slightly. Taking out a compact mirror, she did what she could to even out her skin tone, apply lipstick, and then eavesdropped further, preparing for a cue to exit the building.

"Why didn't you tell me in the first place?" she heard David say.

"Tell you what? There's nothing to tell," Daisy begged.

There was the sound of unnatural movement, a heavy thud and then a scuffle. It startled Trick to action. She bolted out of her bedroom in time to see David dragging Daisy by her hair across the living room and into her bedroom. She sprinted to Daisy's rescue.

As she entered Daisy's bedroom, she saw David sitting on the edge of the bed, Daisy at his feet twisted up in a ball in the floor rug that normally covered the area in front of the main entrance. She was hiding her face behind her hands and tangled hair, the sound of her muffled cries infuriating Trick. David looked up with eyes that sneered, a look that dared to be corrected. His gaze contained more evil than Trick had ever seen that close up before. There was no trace of mercy anywhere on that ugly mug of his. His wicked smile told Trick she was in definite, immediate danger. It took her a few dire seconds to conjure up speech and only then was she able to produce a statement that she knew lacked sincerity. It was more of a simple overture, a strained, tepid plea. "You don't know what this woman has been through. She loves you so much," she croaked and quickly retreated, commencing a blurry search for the phone to dial nine one one. Upon finding it conveniently nestled in its cradle, she got as far as nine when the phone was roughly smacked out of her grasp, the sheer force of the blow knocking it clear across the room.

The voice that filled her ears hit an outrageous pitch, the danger underneath the source bouncing off the sheetrock. "Who the fuck do you think you are? How do you think you got this place?" David was shorter than she was in heels by a couple of inches. She held firm, gazing steady into his ugly, contorted mug, and a feeling of quiet numbness washed over her like a gentle wave on your best

88

beach day. There was nothing she could think to do now because she had stepped into a pile of it. Her calm further unnerved him. He reached out an ink-soaked arm, closed his beefy hand around her neck, and squeezed. She removed herself from anything present, imagined the beach and the breeze. The summer she would spend with her friend Pam in Southampton in their cute bikinis, if only the real heat would arrive. She liked that her friend was older and they could rent a car and stay in a hotel like adults. They would meet men with class who knew how to treat a lady. Her decision to move out was immediate. She knew this was her last night in this crummy place. She felt so much peace as her body was lifted off the ground and her head bashed repeatedly against the far wall, the sound echoing inside her mind each time it connected to the drywall. Then, suddenly, it stopped. Her body fell to floor in a heap and there it stayed, motionless. Darkness surrounded her, her thoughts blackened into a cavernous abyss. Her consciousness found its way back, slowly returning to the throes of a woman's high-pitched scream alongside copious amounts of police filling the room like clowns exiting a clown car. She had never seen so many cops in one place at one time. Someone was lifting her to the couch as she tried to count them and she heard questions being asked of her that she unable to answer because her thoughts and mouth had not yet conspired to work together. She saw through bleary eyes that David was gone and Daisy, face red and washed in tears, was showing the police a picture of her hardened paramour, wearing a bandana on his head in the photo and looking tough as nails, singing on a stage like an aging rock star in all his glory. She knew it was a picture she had coveted, until now.

The sun had apparently gone down, and Trick needed some air. "Can I go outside?" she whispered to the woman in blue closest to her, within her clouded periphery.

"Just a few more questions," the female cop responded.

Trick sat up, finally getting her bearings back. She had little else to add, and when they finally left, Daisy wouldn't stop apologizing. Trick retrieved her purse and left without another word.

The train got in late, but her mother picked her up the same. The ride home was a short distance from the station. Both women remained silent, her mother could sense something was wrong but thought it best to wait for her daughter to speak first. This visit was certainly unexpected. The rain had started an hour ago and there was nobody on the road, which was a good thing because her mother was already a few glasses in. She thought it would be happier times when she saw her daughter next, on a holiday, perhaps. But this would do. It had been too long.

They both held glasses of white wine close to their chests as they curled up on the couch together. The quiet wedged its way into Teresa's soul. She felt isolated after sitting for two hours on that train, talking to no one. She needed to reach out and didn't know how. Her mother broke the ice.

"How are you," she whispered.

"Mom. I don't know."

"It's good to see you."

"Yes," Teresa shifted her position, hugging her knees.

That was it. They sat in silence. The phone rang, summoning her mother into the next room. "Excuse me," escaped her as she left, giving Teresa the opportunity to scurry into the spare room, her old bedroom, pulling the covers over her head and falling into deep sleep, still wearing her clothes. Please don't use this as a reason to get wasted, Ma.

Her mother returned and sat, thinking her daughter would rejoin her. When she didn't, she blew out the candles and went to bed. She slept soundly. She believed inherently that she had taught her daughter well enough and would be there for her when she was ready. She was not one to bully her way into her daughter's business. She worried, of course, but had lived with the knowledge it would be a life-long struggle to fully know this young woman she took a large part in creating. She had raised a freethinking, independent woman and there was much left to be determined.

When Teresa heard the birds, she opened her eyes. From the next room came sounds of rustling. Her mother was preparing breakfast, she assumed. Act lively, she told herself. The fact that she's up means she didn't get blackout drunk last night, so that's a good thing. She gave herself a few more minutes then sat up. Her makeup from yesterday had crusted over, her eyelashes sticky and her skin feeling populated with dirt. She rose and raised her hands in the air, stretching.

She opened the door and sunlight poured in. That's when she heard the music that had been playing all morning. Her mother used to be an early riser and had always loved to keep abreast with everything new that came out musically, songs that had uplifting qualities. The man on the radio was missing some woman who had been his everything. Teresa thought about the irony of a love song, smirking to herself that it took such a loss to create something as beautiful as the ballad that currently filled her ears. Once I was blindly in love, now I can see what I had and lost and doesn't this bridge just clinch it for you. She wiped the corners of her eyes and came up with black goo. As gross as it was, it made her smile. She couldn't remember the last time she woke up in her mother's home, that feeling of being protected because she still had a "home base". It was a nice change of pace because she had spent her years in this house counting the minutes until she could escape it. Her shifting viewpoint made her feel different and freer, as if the nightmare from the previous day didn't matter to the woman that woke up today because things could be made good again. Relief came over her as she danced her way into the kitchen.

"Hey, Mama," Teresa said with a sweet smile.

Her mother turned from washing the dishes to greet her daughter with a sunny disposition, deciding in advance to replace any reservation about her unexplained late night visit with warmth and love. Plus, she had no hangover. She took one look at her daughter and the soapy mug fell out of her fingers and into the sink with a hard crack. "Oh God!" her hand shot up, cupping her mouth with a wet hand to stifle her alarm. Her startled eyes stared, imploringly.

"Mom, what's wrong?" Teresa stopped in her tracks, holding her breath. Her mother walked towards her slowly, mesmerized by her appearance.

"Oh, Teresa," her mother's eyes started to well with tears, as Teresa pushed past her, sprinting to the bathroom. She looked at her reflection in the wall mirror, seeing first her messy, still greasy hair. She was unable to immediately comprehend anything more than a disheveled appearance. Then she

94

saw what her mother was gaping at. On her neck, visible on the front and around the sides and to the back, were enormous, blue and purple bruises. She had never seen anything like it. They covered her entire neck. Whoa, she thought. Wow! She couldn't believe her own eyes. She couldn't move. The effect it produced had her mesmerized as well, as if she were wearing a dark scarf. The violence radiated off of it. This was something that certainly needed explaining and she had no idea what to say for herself, where to start.

"Teresa?" Her mother's voice was tight and nervous. The sound of shoes hitting linoleum approached the door, fingers rapping on the wooded door in a burst. It hurt Teresa's ears to hear it because she was not prepared yet to answer anything. She hadn't even had coffee! Fuck. She ran the water to convey normal atmospheric conditions. There was little time to excuse herself and the thought of getting on the train and heading back into the city this early was depressing, especially since she had nowhere to go, but more importantly, what it would do to her mother. Time to fess up, she realized. So be it. Consequences are par for the course when throw yourself out there in life. There's no escaping cause and effect. She whipped open the door to face her mother head on.

"Mother, I was attacked."

"Oh, my Dear!"

"Yes, it was awful," Teresa clasped her mother's hands in her own and guided her to the kitchen table, sitting her down. "He was very big."

Her mother gave her those worried eyes and Teresa grew sad at how old they looked. She didn't want her mother worrying about her and she certainly didn't want to trigger her mother's drinking. The Trick in her knew she'd be fine, that this was simply a minor snag in the works. Still, she'd have to say something to ease this woman from her protective perch, with the safety from a scary and distracting world found in the myriad of happy birds at their feeders outside the glass windows of the modest home she kept up after the divorce. Her mother had been a sympathetic person her whole life, the eldest of numerous siblings, and that role prepared her to be present to many family dramas. She collected herself and lit a cigarette.

"What happened? Tell me."

"It was nothing, Mama." The last thing Teresa wanted was for her mother to feel

96

bad. How to avoid this was her primary concern. "It was Daisy's boyfriend. Had nothing to do with me, really."

"What did he do to you?"

"I got in the way trying to protect her. He grabbed me. But the cops got him. I'm moving out. Don't worry."

Her mother sat, smoking. Teresa hated seeing her like this, looking down at her hands, her brow furrowed. There was nothing more to say. It all seemed to go nowhere. Anything she thought she could add brought no peace to the situation. If you only knew, Mother. If only you knew what I was really up to, what I'm capable of.

She got up from the table and moved behind her mother and hugged her. There was no return hug, and Trick took that to mean, "You shouldn't have moved to that city in the first place. I taught you better than to align yourself with danger and worry me." But there were no words. She knew how her mother felt. Yet, a mother's concern at this stage was not nearly enough of a deterrent. She would be getting on that train, heading back into the belly of the beast. It was her home now. She was beyond convincing. Anything her mother could come up with was not worse than what she'd already been exposed to. This pity party had suddenly grown tired. Trick needed to move, if she was ever going to find the strength to get back in. She released her hold and moved towards the counter where the coffee pot promised a hot push. "Would you like some more coffee, Mama?" she asked, but knew there would be no answer. Communication, for the day, had ended.

Chapter 4

It's a beautiful, sunny afternoon, the traffic outside the loft window buzzing with activity. Emma returns a newly filled ice cube tray to the freezer, grabs the bottle of Jack on the counter, and quickly pours the whiskey into a glass already with ice. She considers food for a moment, finding the contents of her fridge, various condiments and a single left over metal to go container with the lid popped off, anything but desirable. She waves off the thought, grabbing her drink and returning to her desk to continue typing, immediately engrossed. An ashtray full of cigarette butts is in close proximity. The phone rings several times and she doesn't seem to notice. The answering machine picks up.

"Hey, sis. I don't know. It's a beautiful day. I'm glad you're not home. I hope it means you're out enjoying yourself." The young man on the other end sounds like he is about to hang up.

Emma jumps from her desk, running around trying to find the phone. Tucked into the couch cushions, she scrambles to answer it.

The message continues, "Alright. Well, I'll talk to you later. Loveyoubye."

Emma fumbles to push talk, "Hey, you!"

Emma's brother, Christopher, a tall, dark, and handsome young man of nineteen years, is calling from his sparsely furnished, slightly rundown apartment in a suburb of Suffolk County, Long Island. "Hi, sis! How's it going?"

Emma beams, "It's going! Great to hear your voice!"

"Hammering away at those keys? I'm sure. Listen, I'm coming into the city next week to hang out with the guys. I was wondering if maybe I came in a little early we could have dinner together?"

"Of course! I would love that," she exclaims.

"You're sure you're not too busy?" Christopher asks sincerely.

"You never need to ask me that. I always have time for you. I raised you, didn't I?"

"You wrote a whole book about it," he laughs self-consciously.

"My only best seller," Emma sounds more defeated then she means to.

"But certainly not your last," Christopher knows only too well what to say.

"I don't know anymore. It's been a while. But, there's hope. I can always meet a biohazard to wreck my life like Mom did when she met our father. Lots of good material there."

Christopher is not amused. "I'd rather you didn't," he says flatly.

100

"Right. Sorry," Emma flops on the couch.

"Don't forget, we made a pact to steer each other clear of those ledges."

Emma responds quickly, "I don't want you to worry about me."

"Who else am I going to worry about?"

Emma smiles sadly, "I love you, brother. Thanks for calling." They say their goodbyes and hang up the phone.

4. Under It

Trick doubted herself for the first time today. She was sitting across the desk of a fat man asking questions that started to bother her. He talked about her new duties, simple enough, while she stared out of the office door at the store beyond. A song by The Doors played in her head as she debated this decision to get a job with a modicum of structure, something to make Mama proud. She allowed herself to be lead far enough to be sitting in this tight box with the musty smell of storage and this hairy male, who was foreign and a bit too forward as he overcompensated for cultural barriers. Now, even this exercise in normality grew absurd. Why bother? Five to one, baby, one in five. No one here gets out alive. She cared nothing for retail, except the discount she would receive as an employee. But she questioned the junk she saw, disappointed by the merchandise already. Can't give it away, she thought, and stood, mid-sentence and smiled.

"I've changed my mind. Fuck retail."

He shook his head, offended. She picked up her purse, as well as her stride, and made for the front door. The other sales girls gave her dirty looks that she immediately shrugged off.

It was the freedom she felt walking the streets that she treasured. But the very air repressed her today. Finding meaning for this new conscience had her feeling heavy. Very little made sense after returning from her visit home. What was once a stance at viewing the world as wide open before her now seemed more precarious under the weight of responsibility for her mother's feelings. Why the remorse? Then, the thought of not being good at something, anything, surfaced. Doubt is a killer. Her self-image had taken a nosedive and without the will to pursue a legitimate career, there was little understanding of what was to be done. She was well aware it had been a while since she had traded sex for money and felt she was losing her nerve. She couldn't decide what was important, felt she was drowning, and couldn't figure out how to get out from under.

Anxiety ridden, it was by accident she caught the eye of an ugly man on the street. He was quick to grin and nearly drool in her direction and she felt disgusted by him, that in her weakened state, he expected her to reciprocate his leering at her like a good little chicken. She wanted to punch him. It was awful, having strangers look at her like that. Okay, so I'm having a bad day, she thought. But recognition of the foul mood didn't make it a pill any easier to swallow. She hated when men felt compelled to address her when she didn't address them first. The hate was usurped by how lonely she felt, aware of how completely out of character that was for her to feel. Admittedly, it was time to do something deliberate. Overcoming the mundane idea of getting some menial job and calling it "decent work" failed to deliver any crackle of inspiration. The day was evolving into something useless and she needed something to happen, fast.

She went back to her apartment and Daisy rushed to meet her, offering compliments on a haircut that Trick thought went all kinds of wrong. Something else to be depressed about, she thought. Dropping onto her bed and hoping to let sleep take the pain away, the phone rang.

"Hi-eee," Pam, her producer friend's voice, rang out. "What are we doing?"

"Nothing. I don't feel well."

"You sound like shit. What's wrong, hon?" Pam lit a cigarette and leaned back.

Trick sat up and put her fingers through her shorter hair. "Fabio fucked up my hair."

"Oh, shit. I'm sorry. He always does a great job on me. What happened?" she asked.

"I don't know. I moved?" Trick snickered.

"How bad?"

"Short."

"I'm sure it's fine. You couldn't look bad, sister. But just in case, let me buy you a drink," Pam inhaled smoke.

"Where?"

"You name it. I don't care. Vodka tastes the same everywhere," Pam laughed.

"Can we go to 147?" she asked.

"So that bartender can propose? You really like to torture yourself, don't you. And others. Let's be honest."

"I want to see if any of my clients are around. For later, that's all," Trick looked around the room for her cowboy boots.

"That's complete bullshit. You want to see him again. You forget who you're talking to. But whatever, I thought you were going to stop doing that crazy shit? When are you going to get that out of your head? That shit's dangerous!" There was silence on the end of the line. "Whatever. Convincing you is like trying to pick up a car without the adrenaline coursing through your veins because your baby is trapped underneath. Damn car will not fucking move. Fine. Are you ready to go, or do you need some time to fuss?"

"Remind me again why I'm your friend? See you there in ten," Trick hung up the phone on a laughing Pam. She hoisted herself off the bed and went straight to the mirror, taking in the new look again, trying to recognize the girl she saw looking back with a pained expression behind the eyes. Pam had quickly become her favorite friend and she was counting on her right now to kick-start a different mood. Also, she admitted, she was excited to see that bartender again, although she couldn't figure out why. Something about his eyes piqued her curiosity. All men can't be the same, she guessed. Maybe he held something more than most. She could be wrong about him, but trusted whatever was happening in her gut to carry her there. She was no fool to ignore signs, but didn't dare call it anything yet. She slipped on her boots, grabbed her jacket, and headed out.

Trick passed by a deli with a multitude of different flowers. The colors pulled her out of reverie with their vibrant blues and oranges and pinks. She was sure it would be silly to buy him flowers, but did it anyway. She did it because she wanted to, because it made her smile, and that was enough.

She walked into the dark interior and saw him look up at her with those soft green eyes, resisting the urge to run to him. She needed to calm herself down to avoid appearing eager. But the smile that spread across her face conveyed what she was really feeling nonetheless and she let the feeling

106

flood forth despite her theories on control. She hadn't felt like this before and it was wonderful to be so ready to receive someone's presence. He felt the same. He was glowing.

"I don't even know yer name," he said laughing, as she rushed forward into the half empty bar, throwing the flowers at his face.

"And I, you."

"Jimmy," he said with that gorgeous mouth of his.

"Teresa. Hello," she smiled sheepishly at her forthrightness. For such a bold creature, you're acting like an amateur, she thought. Then it occurred to her, who cares?

"Pleasure," he smiled again, covering his mouth as he did, displaying a shyness that thrilled her. "Can I git you somethin' to drink?'

"Yeah, I don't care. I'm fine," she looked around for Pam, suddenly becoming self-conscious about behaving with such abandon. There were others at the bar looking on, but she met only friendly approval of her impulsive displays of affection. The crowd encouraged more from the two with their open faces. She strangely felt safe.

"Stella?" he asked, grabbing a pint glass.

"No, I don't think so. Something else. Something strong and sweet."

"Like you?" he smiled.

"Oh, good grief," she laughed and looked towards the sound of the front door opening. It was an older couple happily engaged in a dialogue. Trick wondered what it must feel like to really love someone enough.

Jimmy busied himself mixing, then placed a martini glass in front of her and poured a liquid into it that held a reddish-brown glow, plopping in a cherry to top it off. "That's a Manhattan, lassie."

"Don't call me that."

"Try it. You'll love it, knowing ye."

"How do you figure to know me so well, hmm?" she took a sip. "Oh, wow."

"It's called instinct. I've been 'round long enough to know. So have ye, it seems."

"What do you mean by that?" she thought him too presumptuous.

"Nothin'. Sorry. Ye don't have to be defensive with me. Yer company is all I'm after. Yer just my style."

"Shut up. Why would you say that? You don't know a thing about me and you're

108

standing there pretending like you do. It's annoying."

"Yer right. Point is, I'd like to. Get to know ye. Everybody comes from somewhere. And who ye are interests me," his voice had a singsong quality to it.

"Oh, yeah? Why's that?"

"Ye obviously know what ye want. That's rare."

"What are you talking about?" she asked. "Everybody that comes in here wants something out of life. Otherwise, they wouldn't have moved here."

"Yer right, but it's not what I'm referrin' to. Most th' time people are fishin' for somethin', don't always know what. Can't blame 'em. Life's not easy. Always changin'," his eyes lingered on hers for a moment then turned away to make a drink for another customer.

Trick sat still. When he returned she looked at him straight, nothing more. Her confidence skipped a beat. She wasn't sure what to say to him, registering an eventual look of relief for the comfort he provided in the silence between them. He smiled and she loved him for it because it was suddenly very easy. It felt good and nothing mattered. The insecurity that an uncertain life produces, all that troubled exploration, was gone for a precious moment. It felt as if everything was going to be all right. She was grateful to him for making her feel that way. In that same moment, the feeling caused her rough interior to rub. Depending on another would always lead to disappointment, she knew that already. But it was in that still moment her eyes met his, amidst the hum of the surrounding voices of cavorting bar patrons, that her safety net disappeared and she didn't feel the need to brace herself. Things that needed changing would change. And the things she had to get done would get done, without fear. That's what love must feel like, she thought. Love inspires. Jimmy looking at her like that made her feel that those other, seemingly unconquerable things didn't matter because they could, in fact, be conquered. He was the first person to do that for her and it felt glorious.

The next week put a strain on her finances and her heart. Jimmy took her to nice restaurants and asked her what she wanted to be when she grew up and she laughed. She didn't dare divulge how

110

she had been wont to spend her evenings in the past and he didn't seem to want to know. He was easy to talk to and was full of interesting stories, but she didn't yet trust what was happening enough for that much honesty. There were lunches and dinners that filled Teresa with enormous positivity. The two covered significant emotional ground together that ensured the bond between them. But still, she refused to let him pay for her. Mostly, she wanted to represent herself properly. She belonged to no one. Their experiences together certainly deserved the expenditure, and Jimmy didn't put up much of an argument when the bill arrived each time, something she appreciated at first because he recognized her as the independent she was, but then she grew annoyed by it. She wasn't sure when the shift happened in her, but she started resenting him because she wanted him to start treating her like his lady, and it somehow seemed too late for that. She only had herself to blame. Some simple math persuaded her to start thinking about preparing for "work" again, but she had no idea how she could muster the courage to do so and still look Jimmy in the eye. They hadn't slept together yet, but she felt sure it was something he wouldn't approve of.

After changing her clothes numerous times and fixing her makeup twice, she finally stepped outside to hail a cab. She took it uptown to Scores, a strip joint where her friend worked. She was sure to meet a client there, do some business, and return home early to bed before her conscience kicked in. Besides, she loved when her friend danced. There was such freedom and beauty in getting on that stage. Stripping had never occurred to her as an option. She figured it was because she had issues about being that exposed in front of room full of strangers. One stranger at a time was enough for her.

The bouncer had huge arms and a little boy's face. He smiled at Trick as she arrived at the establishment with a staid confidence. He disrupted her cool veneer by wrapping a gigantic hug around her skinny frame. She held her breath as he lifted her up off the sidewalk, and it occurred to her that every time he did this, it was entirely unnecessary. But she played into it because it seemed to make him so happy. The city can be lonely place and

112

familiar faces can bring out the lover in anyone. It wasn't that she was against affection. She had an aversion to appearing adorable and subsequently vulnerable. Anyway, he was a mild obstacle.

"Hey, Balboa. How you feeling?"

"Good. Real good, baby doll," he said warmly, opening the door for her.

Once inside the door, the reception was drastically different. She had learned better than to waste any energy flirting her way into the hearts of the bitches at the front desk. They had spent their earlier days traversing that same stage. Now, discovering they were unable to defy the undeniable fade, they responded to clientele, male or female, always in a strict, businesslike fashion. This was their way of enduring a work night that resulted in nothing more than going home alone to a movie and a pet, the dream of being swept away by their Prince Charming to an uninhabited island with a warm breeze and fruity rum drinks left behind with their youth.

Trick walked straight past the young, thick Italians who were arguing about the cost of admission with the redheaded witch who was not having any part of their negotiations and addressed the perpetually sourpussed blonde who's dye job was waning. "Hi, I'm Trick. I'm here to see Heather."

"She's not working tonight," she snapped, not bothering to look at her clipboard.

"I know she's working. I spoke with her earlier and she told me to come by. Will you please check again?" Trick tried to peer over the top of the list for her name, but the stringy blonde quickly lifted it beyond her field of vision.

"Uh, no. Sorry."

"Thanks," Trick said flatly. She turned to see Balboa step inside.

"You here to see Heather, right?" he asked her.

"Yeah," she said, agitated.

"I saw her come in. She signed in as Pandora."

"Thanks," Trick smiled with gratitude.

She turned and saw that the snotty blonde was giving him a caustic look, and without even checking the list again, she stood her ground. "She didn't sign in with me."

"No wonder. Dealing with you is a pleasure one can live without," Trick said through gritted teeth. She pushed past Balboa and walked out, subsequently aware of the pain in her head. She could

114

pay the troll the thirty-five bucks to cross the bridge, but it was the principle of the thing. She refused long ago to pay any cover, ever. She didn't need to. She was one of them, working the system, and they knew it. That bitch saw the working girl in her from a mile off but denied her entry, her right to make money, even when Heather had definitely put her on the list. The aging blonde's power trip was merciless. Trick left infuriated.

She hailed a cab and cursed the money spent coming all this way uptown. She used her cell phone to call a beautiful transsexual friend, Lativia, who had her pulse on everything there was to do on any given night of the week in the city.

"Hi sweetie!" Lativia's voice buzzed through the phone.

"Oh, honey, where is this cab taking me right now? I need to be surrounded by rich fucks. I need money."

Lativia laughed. "We all do, sweetie. Don't stress. There's a party tonight in a hotel suite, with roof access so we can smoke. Imagine?"

"Where? I just passed 49th street heading downtown."

"Tell him to turn around, hun. 55th and Broadway. The Majesty. Richie will be in the lobby. I'll be there in an hour."

Consequently, a flurry of activity followed and she surprised herself at how often she thought of Jimmy throughout the evening. In the back of her mind she knew he'd be done with work around four. But she resisted running into his arms, fighting the urge to officiate their relationship. She was curious what sex with Jimmy would be like, presuming it would be what others deemed "love making". She hadn't reciprocated his advances nor had she initiated anything sexual for that reason alone. Love was alien to her, love making even more so. Instead, she focused on moving her body to the house music, paying particular attention to the young suit holding court and buying enough champagne for at least a dozen of his newest, closest friends. They danced well together and when a dialogue was finally established, she innocently professed knowing very little of Gucci and Prada and they made plans to go shopping the next day. He would show her the finer things in life and she was thrilled to be given the lesson, displaying the necessary naiveté that
116

only a precarious union such as this could justify. She found herself promising nothing because it wasn't warranted. Therein existed a freedom to play without recourse. Her pussy would go untouched and in turn, she'd made a new acquaintance whose initial proposal promised her material gain for merely facilitating company. Admittedly, she had already given herself over to a sufficient number of knuckleheads in the past, and walking away from those events unscathed emotionally provided proof to herself that she had an ironclad constitution. Things were different now, she thought. Now, she was worth more because somebody out there cared about her. She would merely let this young fuck take her shopping. Why not? She could always return the merchandise for the cash. Money is money.

The situation was rife with complications. There was an underlying uncertainty that this behavior, and her creeping past, would send Jimmy packing. He wasn't safe with the doozy she had in store for him, leaving her feeling like she was blowing in the wind. Sure, he had seen her leave his bar with different guys, different nights. But that could've registered as slut behavior. The girls doing it for money have a whole separate set of Hail Marys.

When she finally returned home that night, there was a message from Jimmy on her home phone. His voice was sweet and soothing and she was dialing his number even before hearing the end of his cooing. He picked up after the first ring.

"I knew it was ye," he whispered.

"Caller ID?" she smirked, pulling off her shoes. The apartment was empty for the week as Daisy was off sailing the blue skies. Trick was happiest under these conditions. Still, it wouldn't last and she owed it to herself to find a new place to live. Even with her ear placed firmly to the ground, finding a decent apartment in New York was a task more difficult than any other in a city with no vacancies. Her patience was being squeezed.

"I felt it."

"Oh really," she began undressing. "What am I doing now?"

"Changin' into somethin' soft and sexy so that ye'll be more comfortable in fer when I come over."

"You're coming over? Wait. Not yet. Too soon," she froze.

"I'm not gonna want to do anythin' ye don't want to do. I just want to see yer
118

beautiful face. I thought about ye all night."

"Me too, Jimmy. But I think..."

"That we should take it slow. Ye said that bit b'fore and I agreed with ye. But look, we're both awake now and maybe I'm speakin' fer myself here, but I'm thinkin' it would be better having ye next to me than thinkin' about it some more. It keeps playin' over n' over in me mind, the smell a ye. I want to be able t' feel yer skin. You have great skin, lassy," he lit a cigarette. "Don't say no ta me right now because it wouldn't be what ye really want. I'm onto ye."

"What are you..." she sat down suddenly.

"Those times ye came inta work. I saw you with those other guys. You were always lookin' at me like you'd rather it were me sittin' there next to ye, not them."

"Well, that's too bad, isn't it?" she said hesitantly.

"Ye got some real fire in ye. Takes a brave girl to work a complete stranger inta takin' ye home with 'em. I'm gonna assume ye sealed the deal with those blokes. Ye gave that impression you weren't 'ccepting anythin' less." Jimmy paused then said carefully, "I don't mind what ye been up to before we met, Teresa. That's not my concern. That's fer you to work out fer yerself. I like what I see in who y'are underneath all that. Yer fuckin' dynamite."

Trick said nothing for about a minute. He smoked in the quiet dark.

"The truth is, Jimmy, I can be very cruel."

"Now that discounts everythin' I just said. Why would ye say that? Do you think that's very nice of ye to take the way I feel about this gorgeous, excitin' creature who dances like a fairy all over my sleepin' and awaken self, and put her down like that? Nah fair. I won't allow it, kiddo."

"Don't call me kiddo," she said curtly.

"Then stop actin' like y'are one."

Trick nearly hung up the phone after that one. But something held her upright. It was the thought of seeing this beautiful Irishman naked, above all else.

"Fine. Come over, then."

"Well, if that's as friendly as ye get. Alright, I accept." He got her address and they hung up the phone. Her nerves decided to stand on edge and jump.

She had little time to change, light some candles, and program her ipod to

120

something moody. He was there in a flash. She opened the door and he moved his body inside the dim room. He looked around, briefly taking in her living conditions and made a joke she didn't like nor understand. He asked her to sit down as he removed his jacket. He chuckled to himself about something. She remained silent because she felt scared that this was certainly not what she had intended, the circumstance constricting her further. She had difficulty breathing and clutched at her stomach because the tension tore a hole in it directly. She climbed on the tacky loveseat and curled her legs underneath her, appropriating a fetal position against all that was terribly wrong with this decision to be among the bleeding hearts of the world. She had succeeded in avoiding the nuisance of it thus far, breezing happily along. Now it seemed she was immersed in the thick of it. Attempting to process what sex with this man could possibly amount to, she developed a tick of moaning.

"It's that bad, is it?" he eased down next to her and took her hand in his. "I don't want to make ye miserable."

He kissed her lips, determined to shed any unwanted sticky stuff, like doubt, figuring they had her held in an aggravated tangle of losses. He wanted to allow her to fly over the life she'd been handed, ready to land hard, and finally feel what it's like to walk with another. There, the purpose of the landlord over a blade of grass reminds the whys they are more important than the whats. The realization that growing up in the solitary proof of burden put upon one's self to deliver all the trust and consideration one could ever need in a lifetime, that in actuality can only come from another, caused a broadening sense of desire in her to explore this new surrender. She hadn't before now realized she secretly wanted someone to really care about how she felt. It was overwhelming, too much a thing to imagine that she could ever feel safe enough to tear down the walls she had defiantly constructed to protect herself from supposed and eventual defeat. And so, against anything appropriating better judgment, she gave in.

He slid off her panties with one hand, the other reaching for her neck to insure her positioning. She made noises of struggle and he teased her. She was highly sensitive to his touch. He unfastened his belt, wore no underwear,

122

and his dick flew out of his jeans, hard. He led her hand to it. She felt its size and that triggered immediacy. She wanted him in her now. Her uncomfortable squirming ceased, and she waited expectantly for him to find his way in. But he waited, feeling her breasts through the thin cotton of her blouse. He found her nipples and rubbed at them, pinched them, and she yelped. He laughed periodically and when she asked him why he was laughing, he replied, "I'm happy," and plunged into her. Her breath held as he moved with her, making everything right and good for once and forever. It was wonderful to be like that, with him. She laughed then, too. Together, they rolled onto the floor and moved as one, honoring the fit and the trigger of his other head inside her. She could come at any moment, but waited. It amounted to pleasure beyond what she'd known before now.

"Thank you," she whispered over and over.

"Oh," he returned the favor by asking for permission.

"What?" she stopped moving, looking into his eyes.

"I'll come in you, but only if you let me."

"Please," she begged.

"Say it again."

"Please. Please, now. It feels so good. Please," she moaned.

And he did, as she did. The event was solidified with a scream that tore out of her, most certainly alerting the neighbors of her imminent death. Her body convulsed and he held onto her until she rode it out, falling limp and exhausted and more relieved than she'd ever felt. He carried her to bed and fell into it next to her. They slept with nothing more than every bit of love, pleasure, and understanding that was needed in this upside down world that was all their own.

A few weeks later, Jimmy surprised her with a trip to Paris. She had no idea how he could afford it, but didn't dare look that gift horse in the mouth. She was packed and ready to go within the hour. She almost didn't believe him until they were boarding the plane.

They spent their first day in bed together. The small hotel was exquisitely furnished but very dark because of the heavy, red curtains covering the windows. They made love for hours, stopping only to eat the delicious, fresh food they picked out at one of the local patisseries. When it was time to step out, she insisted they walk to the arrondissement Pigalle, because she had heard there were women selling themselves via storefronts, as if they were items of clothing to be perused by window shoppers. The thought fascinated her and she needed to see it for herself.

The walk was invigorating. Around every corner was the most beautiful architecture she had ever seen. It smacked of the richness of a culture and a history she had to see to believe. She adored New York, but knew now that Paris was the most beautiful city in the world.

When they crossed over into Pigalle, she sensed it before reading a single street sign. There was something dark about the energy here. It felt naughty and mischievous. They stopped into a sex shop for laughs and discovered in the very back a series of rooms that, upon payment, women would come out and dance behind a glass wall. They picked one and entered its dark interior. A man followed them in and Jimmy used his broken french to communicate they wanted a show, paying him what he asked for. The wall slid open and there stood two women, one considerably younger and prettier than the other, both wearing lacey panties and garter belts, breasts exposed. They danced slowly to an old Parisian love song. Jimmy sat on a small chaise lounge chair, amused at the whole scene. Trick was mesmerized, not at the show itself, a bit sickly and debauched, but at the vulnerability of the older woman, whose body brazenly wore the signs of age. Trick stared, walking up to the glass until her nose almost touched it. As the younger woman straddled a chair in the corner in one of her signature moves, the older woman stopped dancing and slowly approached the glass. She stood directly in front of Trick, holding her gaze. Inside that look held years of struggle and heartbreak. She raised her hand and Trick lifted hers to meet it and they touched, as though the glass did not exist. Tears fell from both women's faces, running makeup over cheeks in silent mourning of life's unnecessary pain.

The building was on fire. The two men had argued with the waitress over the bill, leaving Teresa to wonder why she had agreed to have dinner with them in the first place. They lacked certain class, had embarrassed her, and she

126

wanted out of there. The manager had come over visibly distressed and waived the entire bill. It seemed an all too generous gesture. Teresa scanned the restaurant as it was being evacuated quickly. She grabbed her purse and headed for the stairs. One of the two burly men from dinner saw the open elevator door. The invitation was hard to pass up because the stairwell was jammed with hysterical bodies. He grabbed her and roughly pulled her inside, joining the few nearby who took the same chance and lost. As the door closed behind them, the already dim lights flickered and they heard the cable snap. They clung to the sides as they hung by the remaining cable soon to melt and dissolve, their remains sure to plummet down the shaft and into the nothing below. They huddled in shock, looking at one another with wide eyes, still as glass. There was no hoisting anyone towards a rescue trap door up above. They were dangling. No one moved. The screaming continued outside the sealed door and Teresa looked around wildly, feeling nauseous. Anyone in their right mind knew in case of fire use stairs. They hadn't heeded that universal axiom and now it was a matter of moments before she would have to welcome her

demise. Strangely, she didn't feel fear. It had enveloped her and she became one with it, until a voice filled her ears. It had a deep register, rich in its delivery of a message that surrounded the insides of her skull. Did anyone else hear this? She crouched low, her eyesight growing dark, her hearing muted except for this rich sound that encompassed her fully. She could do nothing but pay attention to it. It said something to itself and laughed. In that laughter was pie and whiskey, warm and inviting. It said, "Well, here we are. Good. There is no heaven, you know. Only this. You'll enjoy spending time with me, I can assure you. Wonderful having you." She knew who it was then. She looked around and saw that the panic in the faces of the people in elevator was in response to their extreme conditions, but not to the voice. No, she was the only recipient of its dark message. She called it the devil, assigned its identity, and immediately cast it gone. She said to it, "I'd rather there be no god and be dead forever than side with you. You don't get me!" The maniacal image behind the voice, slitted eyes and a mouth lined with a hundred teeth, flew roughly out of her, as an abortion is ripped from a woman in those
128

fateful moments the vacuum takes hold of the denied cargo. It flew above her body, faces almost touching, and slithered above and away from her. She shuddered at its fast and angry departure. She managed to feel proud of her courage and braced herself to face the inevitable aftermath that would follow.

It wasn't until this moment of the morning, waking from a dream that threatened to splatter her ruins, through a haze that hadn't been washed away by sleep, that the horrible events of the night before were delicately recounted. "Shit," she murmured, as she opened her eyes and registered that Jimmy was not there, in fact had not opted to go home with her because he wouldn't dare sleep next to the lunatic she had proven herself to be last night. It was difficult remembering what had happened, exactly. There were waves of shame and disgust in the flashes that her brain allowed regarding the prior evening's debacle.

Could she rise? What time could it possibly be? Lack of direction drove her back under, but only for a short minute. Of course she had to get up, had to rectify the catastrophe. She could sense it was bad, even if she couldn't remember any of it. I wish I may, I wish I might, she whispered. Why? I know, she thought, it's going to be ok. What do you know? Obviously not much, she gathered. Get up! Fuck off, my head hurts. Food, please. Stomach hasn't seen food in too many hours.

Teresa peeled herself off her sheets, naked, stumbling for the bathroom. She couldn't remember if Daisy was home or not. There was little energy to expend caring at this point, even if David The Evil Boyfriend decided to resurface and rape her scrawny ass. She only had concern for emptying her bladder and calling Jimmy.

Her peeing was tinged with a burn from the day before. They had fucked especially hard and she loved the way it felt, her pussy all torn and utilized. But then a flash of memory, the sound of his voice, played in her head. "Ye don't get my cock," he'd said it in anger. She wiped her delicate privates and shuffled her feet towards the answering machine. It had no new messages. Neither did her cell phone. She reviewed last night's calls and saw an outgoing call clocked at 4:36 a.m. to Jimmy. They went to Pangaea, a nightclub filled with sexy beauties, and she recalled a fistfight between her and Jimmy, with a crowd to confirm and later judge. That could explain the finger that was sore and wouldn't straighten. The more she examined it, how swollen it was, the more she panicked. The pain when she squeezed it alerted her it was, in fact, broken. She heard Jimmy's voice, pleading with her to calm down. "Don't tell me what to do. You won't win," she remembers saying. Why? She forged ahead, ripping his shirt off of him for talking to another woman. It all sounded so crazy. She crushed the guilt into a more manageable lump, to discard from a quickly moving cab, if only he would take her call. The morning was a storm.

She racked her brain, trying to remember. Her friend Pam, who was always up for a good time, had joined them very late in the course of the evening. By then, Teresa was already very drunk. Because Pam got a late start to the evening, she would have retained more and would be able to fill in the gaps, right? She called Pam pronto.

"Yeah?" Pam answered in a voice consumed with sleep and smoke inhalation from the previous night's escapades.

"Pam honey."

"What the fuck's wrong with you?"

"What happened?" Teresa was prepared to beg.

"You freaked out. I wouldn't be surprised if he never talked to you again."

"I think I have a broken finger," Teresa said absently.

"The way you were going at him, I was sure he'd break your face. I had to get out of there."

"You left me?" Teresa was shocked.

"You were scary! What do you expect?"

"Should I call him?"

Pam rolled over in bed and lit a cigarette, "You should call somebody. I don't know what to tell you,"

"Don't say that. You're my best friend."

"Now you say that. Last night you were calling me an asshole. I thought you were going to hit me!" Pam sighed. "Listen, I know you were drunk, but come on. What the fuck."

"What was I drinking, anyway?"

"Whatever you could get your hands on. You were grabbing people's bottles off their tables. I've never seen you like that before," Pam paused. "Are you ok?"

"I think so. Except for my finger."

"Come over. I'll fix it and make us some food. Then you can call your man, but not a minute sooner. And no name calling."

"Thank you. I love you."

"Yeah, sure. You're still drunk," Pam joked.

Teresa hung up the phone and swayed with vertigo getting into her jeans. She grabbed her keys and wallet and headed out. She had to re-enter the apartment to retrieve her cell phone, cursing the day as she tripped over the coffee table, guaranteeing a nice bruise on her knee. What the fuck did I do? She wondered.

She climbed the five-floor walkup to Pam's apartment, reasoning with each searing bolt of pain in her head that there'd be solace found up these concrete steps, her reward for making it up this punishing path. Besides, Pam made a fabulous Bloody Mary and she needed something to calm her frayed nerves.

She rapped on the front door with her good hand and heard her friend moving about inside. The sound of the door being unlocked caused a rush of momentum as she twisted the knob with force, forgetting the injury to her finger and letting out a yell. Bad to worse.

"Get over here, you head case," Pam looked as haggard as Teresa felt and she managed a quick kiss and a one-armed half hug. More than likely, Teresa looked worse, but there was no time for being vain when she had hurt the people closest to her. The friends made their way into the bright kitchen where Pam took on the task of cutting strips of paper tape.

"I'm sorry. I'm so sorry," Teresa had her head down, talking into her stomach.

"Fine, that's the last apology you get to make. You know what they say about how love means never having to say you're sorry?"

"Yeah, I never understood that," Teresa said.

"Why does that not surprise me? It means you never do something to someone you love that requires an apology. Get it?" Pam began setting Teresa's right middle finger. "You're a real shit, you know that?"

"I need to know what happened," Teresa protested.

"You don't remember any of it?"

Teresa let out a heavy sigh. She shook her head.

"Ok. I'll tell you," Pam clucked her tongue throughout the entire process of
134

wrapping the finger, but Teresa let the reprimanding slide, absolutely. She was in no position to thwart anything directly or indirectly. She was left to turn her animosity inwards. She had relinquished the upper hand to her friend. That was punishment enough. Teresa hated having to play the submissive, wounded bird.

They settled onto the purple, velvet couch with their drinks. Pam made them extra spicy to give the morning the kick it required. Teresa's cell phone remained inactive by her side. She was looking at it constantly, as if it had rung and she hadn't heard it. Pam took note, but said nothing. Instead, she spared some kindness. "How are you feeling?"

"I am better than I was an hour ago. Thank you."

"How did you sleep?" Pam said, draining a large portion of the glass. She got up to grab the pitcher she had made of the convoluted substance, swimming in horseradish.

"I dreamt I met Satan and told him to go fuck himself."

"Right on. That's the way," Pam laughed.

"Ok, just tell me. What did I do last night?"

"Oh, sister. Jimmy was talking to some girl and you freaked."

"Who was she?" Teresa asked, drinking.

"Who knows? But you seemed to forget that he loves you because you handed the girl her ass. Then, you turned on him. You went swinging."

"How'd I get home?"

"I couldn't tell you. Maybe you should stop drinking," Pam chimed and they both guffawed. Pam helped herself to some more of the red concoction on cue, Teresa downing most of hers to make room for the next offering from the gamy pitcher.

It wasn't too much longer that Teresa felt the need to make the call. It was almost noon and her head was swimming enough to know that to continue drinking would only create more friction in the memory department. Already, new doubts found their way in, impeding progress when she needed to be as coherent as possible. She felt almost confident she could craft a favorable argument, if only she could stave off the unraveling she felt in her chest to keep the conversation steady. State your case. Ease him in with honesty to a place that's loving and forgiving, and they'd be together in a matter of an hour. She didn't want to be without him, surely. But

136

something had sent her over the edge and she needed to be absolved. Pam hadn't been able to offer up too much in way of details. But she had proven a safe haven after the shit storm that was last night, the true definition of a friend. Except, of course, that Pam had left her behind when she should have pulled her drunk ass out of there. She'd take up issue with that at a later date. No sense in starting a fight with the only friend she had right now. Pay back would be a fabulous bitch, though. She thought of her friend's aversion to heights and it made fine sense to take her to Great Adventure, buy her gastric food and force her on a scary ride or two. She was all about confronting fears at this point, hence the dialing of the number. What else would there be in her life? It was formulating itself to be one of trysts and tests and if she didn't allow her slip to show from time to time, she wouldn't fully realize the force she had been born with, one that demanded one life to be lived fully at no one else's expense, not even her own. Go. And so, she went. Anyone who tried to take away her joy, she'd stick it in their ass.

"Hello," Teresa was easy in her delivery, soft and gentle. She lay fully stretched out on the purple couch. Pam busied herself with cleaning up the breakfast dishes, bagels with cream cheese, day old salmon and capers. After Teresa had finished reprimanding her friend for leaving her, she vowed to do something nice for her to thank her for caring. Pam's company helped to return a semblance of peace, as friends do.

"Hey," he answered the phone, a very good sign that the battle was half won. His voice sounded groggy, that gorgeous time of the morning when he'd fight her for ten more minutes. He could sleep his way through a parade. It was something she allowed because of her attraction alone to his beautiful, sleepy eyes and the soft skin of his shoulders and back. She would giggle through his protests, touching and smelling and licking when he hated to be disturbed. He did play hard to get sometimes and that brought her coming back even harder. It was ok to show desire for your partner once the deal was made, or so she thought.

"I'm not sure what that was, and, you know, I think I must be very sorry," she started to laugh at how ridiculous she sounded. Please, now that I have renounced Satan, allow goodness to shine down on this mess with the grace that my
138

sterling sincerity warranted. She stopped laughing. "I'm straight up right now."

Jimmy was quiet. That was the moment when she felt her world change. Because it was in that moment of her exposing that precious vulnerability she had protected her whole life that he chose to be the "bigger" man and say, "Yeah, sure. Whatever."

Her heart sank. She struggled to speak, "Uh… What? I mean, maybe you could shed some light on the subject. How'd that be?"

"Yer up?"

"Yeah," she said, hating the obviousness of the question.

"Oh," he said. And that was all.

She sat upright. The flavor of that purple couch no longer lavender but grape stain. She had been feeling good since Pam took her in, as if the world was not really against her. But now, the comfort she felt slithered away. She needed to know not only what had happened, but what it meant to him. And, "Who the fuck was that woman?"

He coughed and spit and shifted position. "Me wife," he mumbled.

"Your what?" her words came out of her throat like vomit. She immediately felt as if the ground had fallen out from underneath her, taking with it any kind of love or trust she had for this man, before or after this moment, in one fail swoosh, and was forced to acquiesce to more of this brand of pain for the sake of hearing the truth.

"I'm married, Teresa," his words hit her like a blunt object.

"Oh, ok. Well, I thought I was your girlfriend," Teresa stared at the ceiling at nothing.

"Yeah, well, I live with this one. She just got back into town."

Silence.

"I think you must be a real fucking asshole," Teresa edged out.

"We were separatin'. I didn't expect her to come back."

"What," she couldn't even think past that.

"We were havin' problems. Why would I tell ye about her when I didn't think she'd come back? She showed up at the place and we were workin' through it and you reacted. Violently. I know it's not yer fault."

Teresa laughed. She hung up a hundred times before she spoke next. "I wish you both the best," she said through thick mire.

140

"You're really somethin' special. You know that, right?"

"Sure am." Pushing 'END' on her phone was as easy as engaging the brake pedal at a red light. Well, that takes all, she thought. She stared straight ahead, tossing the phone off to the side of the room with a crack, the battery disengaging and separating itself from the body.

Pam came into the room and stared. "What happened?"

"Nothing. I'm going," Teresa gathered her phone in pieces, kissed her friend, and left. There were no words passed. Sometimes, friends know when to say no fucking words.

Chapter 5

Emma stumbles down the dark, cobblestone streets of Soho, smoking a cigarette with her head down, lost in thought. She looks up to confirm the entrance to Raoul's and stamps out her cigarette, clumsily. She straightens her back and walks inside.

Emma approaches the young and very pretty hostess, dressed to the nines in the day's fashion. Emma pulls her worn shawl closer to her arms and struggles to be heard over the noise of the busy restaurant, "The reservation is under Scott."

"Yes, Ma'am. He's not here yet. Would you like to sit at the bar and wait? We can only seat complete parties," she says condescendingly over the roar of restaurant patrons.

Emma snaps, "No, I don't want to sit at the bar. I want to sit at our table. If I were dining alone, would you seat me? Let's pretend I'm eating alone. Do you want me to pick a table for myself or are you going to do your fucking job and seat me?"

The pretty hostess, not wishing to cause a scene, says quietly, "Very well, Ma'am. Right this way."

"Ma'am," Emma snickers under her breath and follows.

The hostess leads Emma to her seat as fellow patrons regard her entrance. She takes her seat and roughly taps on the hostess' long, lithe arm. "Please tell my waiter I want a double whiskey, neat." The hostess nods her head, but not before rolling her eyes, and walks off. Emma gingerly pushes hair off of her face. The waiter approaches the table with menus and Emma's drink. She drains half the glass and continues to wait, uncomfortably. After an indiscernible amount of time, she finishes the glass.

James finally enters the restaurant and immediately flirts with the pretty hostess. She giggles and points out the table where Emma is sitting. He saunters over and leans in to give her a kiss on the cheek. She responds coldly by turning away from the kiss. He takes his seat. "Well, hello to you, too," he mutters.

Emma cuts to the quick, "You're late."

"Don't start," he unfolds his napkin and places it gently on his lap, grabbing a menu.

Emma gives him a long, hard stare. Her voice rises as the booze starts to kick in, "James, I used to think I was the somebody. In fact, I was. But only because I had accomplished something people deemed important. People gave a shit about me. And then, they didn't. People were dropping me when I thought I was the one ignoring them. You arriving late painfully reminds me of that. It tells me my time isn't valuable to you."

"Oh, are you going to take me to Crazy Town right now? Because last time I checked, I got off that train. You know, the coin flips and it doesn't always come up heads. You want people to care about you? Try giving a shit about them! You've spent the last ten years getting

144

drunk over past success and failures. You alienate yourself on purpose. It's your own fault! No one is telling you to live like a hermit, Emma. When the hell are you going to stop torturing yourself?"

"Expectation causes anxiety. You should try writing a book sometime."

"You're thinking too much about the reviews before they're even written."

"I have to keep writing the way I want to write. I don't need you, or anybody else judging me."

The waiter approaches the table. He asks reluctantly, "May I get you something, Mr. Scott?"

James smiles brightly, "Yes! I'll have a bottle of sparkling water."

"Right away, Sir."

The waiter begins to walk away, but not before Emma grabs his arm. "Hello! I'm sitting here, too! I'll have the same, thank you very much," she shakes her empty glass in his direction.

"Of course," the waiter's scoff does not go unnoticed.

Emma grows aggravated, "James, if I fail again, people will congratulate themselves on their foresight. Do you realize how difficult my job is?"

James sighs, "Ah, Em. We've gone over this before. You would be one of the few to have a New York Times best-seller twice. And I would take great pleasure in being the instrument through which that was achieved. Stop making me out to be the bad guy."

"You walked out on me. You know how difficult this is for me, and you left. And now I'm stuck in a world that's depressing the fuck out of me. What hope am I able to pass along to this woman in my book when the men continue to suck in this one?"

James leans in, "How about we hop on a plane and finish this conversation in the Bahamas?"

"Please, I have enough fiction in my life," Emma laughs, despite herself.

James laughs. The waiter returns with their drinks. Emma takes a long swig. James holds up his glass. "So, let this be your pity party. Come on, let's order. I'm starving," he grabs a menu.

"Your professionalism towards my work has fallen short, to say the least. I need your notes asap. I'm all alone with this."

"Look, I'm pressing ahead. I'm in the office every day at nine. We punch two different clocks, Emma. And at the end of the day, it's all about what's accomplished. In this case, not what the reviewers say but how many books you sell. And I've got my hands full of new talent. Don't play the needy card with me. Get it done. It's not like you're going to heed any of my notes

146

anyway. I came here tonight to let you know someone out there still cares," he throws the menu down onto the table.

Emma looks up at the ceiling, "Are you still on the clock?"

"That depends. What did you have in mind?"

Emma grabs her drink and feigns throwing it at him. He ducks and a look of disgust crosses her face. She takes a drink instead. "Did you even read what I sent you? I left you three messages this week," she exhales loudly.

James throws his hands up in the air. "I haven't had the time to finish. Nice resurrection of the word milquetoast, by the way. Thought that word died and went to lexicon heaven," he smiles. "I'll get to it this weekend."

"You know what I resent the most? That fact that you crack the whip to get me writing, I work my ass to the bone, then you don't bother keeping your end of the bargain. You've had my next two chapters for a week. You know how hard it is for me to go on without your notes. Why do I feel like I'm not interesting enough for you anymore? Because we already fucked? James, you represent me. You're my fucking agent. So act like it and do your fucking job," Emma stands up, a bit wobbly. "Don't forget, I'm the one who put YOU on the map," she finishes her drink, slams the glass down on the table, and walks out of the restaurant.

James remains at the table, still.

A tired, messy looking Emma sits at a proper kitchen table in an immaculate Upper East Side apartment. The kitchen is bright white with the morning sun and has a bleached quality due to repeat cleaning. The blonde woman sitting opposite her is very well manicured. Her white, silk blouse is buttoned to the top and her slacks are neatly pressed. They are around the same age, both look older but for different reasons. A small boy plays at the blonde woman's feet as she answers Emma's questions.

"Who was Donnie to you?"

"He saved my life. If it wasn't for him, I wouldn't have been able to get off the drugs. He gave me the means to get out of town and away from all the chaos and get my head back on straight. I owe my life to Donnie," the blonde woman rubs the boy's head playfully. Emma is hunched over, scribbling diligently onto her yellow pad with one hand, supporting her pounding head in the other.

5. Up and At 'Em

A chance encounter with a billionaire aligned Trick with her next place of residence. She met him in a restaurant and he took a liking to her immediately. She played aloof because she could while he extended his

148

connections because he could, both parties knowing their roles within the context of the ruse. The result was a small studio apartment in a doorman building in Midtown Manhattan. She refused money from this rich guy because she figured friends like him come only so often and she wanted him to see her for her true potential to accomplish something great, that desire far surpassing a roll in the hay. Teresa was more than happy to sleep on the single mattress that was plopped in the middle of the empty room, surrounded by all her books. She had never stopped reading, despite everything. Men and money entailed sacrifice, and both were notorious for coming and going. Her life was so up in the air that it didn't matter. She knew she could count on her favorite writers Faulkner, Coelho, McCarthy, and Hesse to see her through the winter. One paragraph could make her anxious for hours, as if maybe she could manage to step aside her chaotic life and let herself become something bigger than herself. The books provided the grey, stormy days with immense clarity of thought.

She was up against definitive odds. Yet, despite pushing the arduous wheel barrel of working for others, she returned to great minds to form reason for compromise. She was learning, philosophically, that there was a better way for people to consider themselves, as they were, honestly rooted in the comfort found when one trusts oneself. She gathered long ago that selling yourself short was for the feeble minded and she collected strength in this new quiet that she was in fact worth more, amidst the probable misfortune that we all may very well end up unrealized. Without opportunity fastened, the greatest of minds and the most talented of artists can likely be lost or stolen like a stone that's been painted blue and tossed into the ocean, ne'er to be discovered, the travesty of that echoing the ages.

And so she shifted, attending to herself and less to others with the simple act of not giving up her time so easily. Suffice it to say she had only herself to count on, once again, and she felt comfortable there. Years ago, she had wanted desperately to end the day with kind words from a trusted other, but she supplanted those feelings by talking herself to sleep, kindly. She had become something else, something unplanned. She loved and mourned every minute of it. She
150

kept most things heart-felt at a distance. There was plenty of silence surrounding her, as the choice was made every day to remove things that were extraneous. Cut the fat. She knew only what felt good and right now the quiet protected her from more confusion. She shut her phone off most days.

There came a Friday after a long week of contemplation when desire to get out of her head and do something different demanded she attend a party on a yacht that was docked at the Chelsea Piers, setting out for a night cruise across the Hudson. The invitation came from a friend she bumped into at her local deli, since she rarely left her neighborhood anymore. At first, the idea held no interest for her. But, she came to her senses when she realized she hadn't changed her clothes in almost a week. Her appearance was starting to look like the homeless guys she continued to play chess with in the park, perhaps with a little less fervor. Life had gotten harder.

The truth was, the last time she had stepped out to "work", some guy she met on the street propositioned her for an entire weekend of "snuggling", for a hefty price, and she struggled with the

151

temptation. It had been long enough since her breakup with Jimmy, but for some reason, the prospect made her nervous. She got by doing odd jobs here and there, mainly service related, while conveniently ignoring the cringe factor at how remedial it all seemed. She sought solace in her books and that comfort seemed to chip away at her courage to go through with that whole act. Now here she was, agreeing to have dinner with this guy at a trendy restaurant for the sake of good, free food with the promise for more down the line. But halfway through the meal, she excused herself to use the restroom because she was growing uncomfortable in his presence. He was pompous and loud and made her nervous. Exposing herself to the danger inside that risk somehow lost its appeal when she began to think she was worth more than this. He followed her into the bathroom of this nice restaurant and pressured her into giving him a blowjob. He had his dick out and started stroking it before she had a chance to register what was happening, or to protest, and he told her she was driving him wild and that he was so close to coming, begging her to help him with his orgasm. She did just that to get him the hell out of the ladies room before they were detected. Overall, it was sloppy because she was preoccupied the whole time with the thought of getting caught. After he came in her hair, he threw several twenty-dollar bills at her feet, zipped up his pants and left her alone to soak in the humiliation. At least now I can buy groceries, she thought.

The boat ride seemed exactly what she needed to get her mind off of things. She decided on crisp, white linen from head to toe and felt pleased with the freedom of movement her billowy clothes allowed. She grabbed a cab and set out. She knew a few people that were going and looked forward to ridiculous banter from the men and women who lived for the moment, avoiding conversations about their inevitable futures. It didn't matter. At this point, her social skills had waned. She knew she was missing something, holing herself up the way she had been doing. Jimmy had broken her heart, when she promised herself to never let that happen. But her wheels were spinning and her mind needed to be appeased with external stimulation. Sitting at home sulking was no longer working for her. She had mourned long enough.

The day presented promise. The boat was nearly full by the time she arrived, those already onboard were looking bright and ready for action. Pretty fancy, she thought, and almost turned around. Be fearless, she thought, and boarded. Even before the big boat left the dock, the festivities were well underway. There were long tables of fresh sushi and fruit that looked prettier than anyone wanted to eat. This crowd seemed more interested in drinking their dinners. Tables lined one side, where people were already helping themselves to droves of champagne and some were dancing to the music being pipe-lined throughout the boat. Moods were high without any real reason for the party but to celebrate life and to the living of it. She ran into the guy who invited her and joined his table, introducing herself to many, and forgetting names in all the excitement. Her friend asked her if she wanted some ecstasy. She had never tried it before and thought, why not. They popped the pill together and she took a deep breath. Here we go!

As the night wore on, her friend eventually disappeared from sight and she wandered aimlessly through the
154

upper and lower decks, looking for anyone she recognized, feeling both lost and out of place. She resigned herself to smiling politely a lot, but saw no familiar faces. It left her with a lonely feeling amidst such fabulousness but she refused to have a bad time, pressing forward until she acquainted herself with a group of cool looking kids who were laughing and teasing each other and talked nothing of importance and smoked a lot and were nice to her. She imagined the pill was kicking in because the music suddenly got better as she began shaking her hips, despite herself. Onlookers encouraged her and they all laughed together. She felt decidedly excellent.

About an hour into the trip, a torrential rainstorm came out of nowhere and scared the passengers into hiding on the lower deck below. The rain refused to let up, progressively getting worse until the yacht, unable to see much of anything and the condition of the captain's motor skills questionable at best, made too sharp at turn and caught some turbulent waves, causing half of the luminous bottles to slide off the bar in a cacophonous crash of glass and booze. Women screamed. Teresa felt ill, and made her way back to the upper deck for air. The rain was relentless, as was the trance-like house music throughout. She carefully tiptoed her way to the open dance floor, being pounded by rain from the angry gods above. She was getting drenched and didn't care. It felt too good on her skin. She danced unabashedly, feeling the water soak through her white linen and down her bare arms. She squeezed her eyes shut and tilted her face up to the sky to receive more of it. She laughed as she pushed forward her tits and hips, the most prominent features of her thin frame. She had nothing on her mind and not anything to worry herself over, the rain exorcising the malcontent from within her. She felt gorgeous. When she finally opened her eyes, she saw there were four others sharing in that glory, a tall, handsome swinger from Sweden, a beautiful brunette exhibitionist from Queens who's bare tits were flying high, a player from Montreal with a fedora and heartbreaking smile, and a man with short, cropped hair and tattoos covering his forearms. Each found their own spot on the dance floor to call their own, moving instinctually in orchestrated harmony. Without words to convey how

156

good they felt, they continued to dance through their soaked clothes until the big boat docked, feeling sure they had been among kindred spirits. So what if people were staring? She felt sure she had landed onto something real. They were the only people on earth that ever mattered in all of existence. Pure reckless abandon.

When the boat finally docked, Teresa got lost in the shuffle afterwards as people scrambled for their dates. It didn't matter to her, really. She was born alone, early and small and incubated for weeks, and accepted in her heightened state that she would die alone and that everything would be okay. Not one person she met in this life would ever take her place when that day came. With that, she forgave everyone and looked for the next elevation. Hallelujah! She turned to see the tall, blonde Swede standing there with his stunning model wife. They both towered over her and that made her giggle. She was overjoyed to exchange numbers with the couple. They were both so kind and loving to her and she told them she would pay them a visit in the days to come.

Their Soho loft was filled with paintings and throw pillows, color and light and sound. He offered her tea and while his wife fretted about something or other, Teresa noticed he had an enormous chessboard eclipsing a low coffee table in the corner of the vast room. She asked him if he would like to play and it was game on.

After letting him win the first game, as was her signature move, he was incredulous that he was unable to beat her again. Game after game, the pieces were set up and knocked off just as quickly. Teresa was delighted at his determination. Then, in the middle of a game that looked as if he might actually take her down, the wife interrupted them to ask if they had any interest in going out the Hamptons to attend a party being thrown by a old rich guy named Donnie. The Swede hopped in his seat. "You have to see his house! It's right on the beach and it's absolutely gorgeous! Donnie knows how to throw a proper party. You'll love it!"

They decided to bring the game with them, as the Swede agreed to go only if they could continue playing. This made Teresa laugh. "Of course. A wonderful idea!" she said. They marked their pieces, packed the game, and took the car Donnie had sent for them all the way out to
158

Eastern Long Island. On the ride there, she came to learn that Donnie had made all his money slinging carpet for low, low prices. His chain of stores became famous for their spokesman, who would yell directly into camera with some kind of freak of nature enthusiasm, full voice and sweating. It was a ridiculous campaign, Teresa remembered it well, but it did make the old guy a semi-celebrity and donned him with enough wealth to host a battalion of available young things at his house for not just one night of rabblerousing, but an entire week of unbridled debauchery.

The house was more beautiful than she imagined from their description. It seemed to have more rooms and wings than anyone could count. The kitchen was packed with a full staff busily preparing a late lunch for hungry partygoers. Out back, the pool was littered with beautiful faces, the grassy area on the side of the house hosted a volleyball net, where tan, fit men and women showed off what their bodies were made of. Mostly, the game involved a lot of flirting.

The Swede had no shame dragging his enormous chessboard through the party, and Teresa admired him for that. They chose two empty chairs down by the pool and set up their game. Whether or not he was beating her back at the loft, he was smoking her now. She blamed the numerous distractions surrounding them, but refused to give up. That's when she heard the voice, deep and gravely, behind her. It was meant exclusively for her, it seemed. It said, "Can I give you some advice on your game?"

She whipped her head around, her frustration turning to anger that anyone would have the gall to disrupt her focus specifically and their game at large. There, about ten feet away, sat the master of the house. It had to be him. His big brown belly roasted in the sun as he lounged back on a swanky pool chair, eyes closed, flanked by two beautiful women on either side of him, both in skimpy bikinis and shiny from lotion. Teresa rose, and marched over to him directly and said in his ear so no one could hear, "If I take your advice, and I win, I'm sitting next to you at dinner tonight."

He gave her the kind of advice that showed her he had been paying careful attention, offering up strategy she'd failed to notice because she was too wrapped up in everything going on

160

around her and too keen on winning the game. She took his advice and won, the Swede cursing his head off. She turned to thank him, but he was gone.

That night, the crew attending dinner was mighty. They nearly took over the entire restaurant. Teresa's eyes landed on the big guy at the head of the table and saddled up next to him. They all took their seats. Everyone was young and beautiful and having the time of their lives. Teresa, however, spent her time picking Donnie's brain. With each bite, they grew fonder of each other. He liked her wit. She adored his intelligence, his business savvy, and his nerve. He didn't give a fuck what anyone thought of him. He lived his life to the fullest and made those around him happier for it. He was a man of leisure who spread his wealth to others, seemingly without regrets. She admired him thoroughly.

Back at the house, people dispersed for their own enjoyment. Some went night swimming, while others took a walk on the beach. Donnie introduced Teresa to a beautiful young girl and led them into his master bedroom, then excused himself. The beautiful girl took her clothes off and jumped into bed. Teresa followed, rolling around the freshly laundered sheets with her, kissing and groping each other until others began entering the room. Teresa didn't want to appear as if she was putting on a show, moving off to the side of the room as everyone began disrobing and piling into the bed. Teresa was shocked with the reckless abandon the others shared, licking and sucking and fucking each other. It was like watching a car wreck, impossible to turn away. She saw men having sex with other men missionary style, unaware that men could have sex that way. She always imagined it going in from a doggy-style position. Donnie caught her attention from across the room and led her into his gigantic walk-in closet, where he offered her a line of cocaine off an immaculate marble surface. She acquiesced and suddenly felt vulnerable and exposed. She grabbed her clothes and got the hell out of there, leaving the throes of hedonism in her wake. It was too much for her newly discovered fragile sensibilities to take. Oh well, she thought, I'm not as free about these kinds of things as I thought. Which was fine for her budding pursuit of something more. Prudishness did not count her out of the race. In fact, it

162

made her feel more valuable than these
careless sluts.

Chapter 6

Emma sits at a big booth by herself and slowly eats her breakfast while reading a newspaper. The waitress walks by with a pot of coffee, "Can I get you anything else?"

Emma answers without looking up from the paper, "Yeah, I'll have some more coffee." The waitress fills her cup and walks off. Emma continues to pick at her food, slowly turning the pages of the paper back and forth without reading them, her impending visit that evening distracting her from her work on the book.

Sitting at her laptop later that afternoon, Emma stares blankly at the screen. She flips through the pages of her yellow pad, the words found there going in one eye and out the other. She closes the pad, looks at the time, and heads for the shower, albeit a tad early. She's too distracted to pay attention.

The Sidewalk Café in the East Village serves up the kind of cooking that can make anyone homesick. Emma chose it for that reason. She sits writing in her yellow pad as she waits for Christopher's arrival. She stares off towards the street at nothing in particular. Her fingers play with the cap end of her gold and black antique fountain pen.

As Christopher approaches the café, he yells out to Emma while walking into oncoming traffic. She smiles at the sight of him, but a speeding cab that barely misses him impedes her view. There is a loud beep of the cab's horn as Christopher jumps out of the way to avoid being hit. Emma's face drops, as does the pen in her hand. He appears on the other side of the cab, with a large, goofy grin on his face. He recovers from the close call with a skip and a jump, throwing his arms in the air.

Emma sighs relief and stands to greet Christopher. They embrace in a prolonged hug. "I thought I taught you that lesson already," she manages through her offset nerves.

"I forgot. Is it look left, right, then left again?" he snickers, taking the seat closest to Emma's and they both sit down.

"Please don't scare me."

"How do you like my new shirt?" Christopher thumbs at the collar.

Emma smiles, "You always look great, honey."

"You talk to that guy about a summer job for me yet? You know, something not too demanding that pays well. I don't want to get up too early and I don't want work late. Or think too much."

"Why not become a writer? Make your own hours, collect checks. A great life," she says sarcastically.

166

"You know, I thought about that. But then it'd probably end up being a shallow book of one-liners. I don't have much to say, sis. I'm not like you."

"Breaks my heart," she says, smiling.

Christopher leans back in his chair as his attention slips away to the very sexy waitress who approaches their table to take their drink order.

"Can I get you anything to drink?" she asks, making eyes at Christopher.

"Yes, I'll have a double shot of whiskey with ice. In a rocks glass," Emma answers coolly.

"I'll have a screwdriver please. And thank you," his grin is all teeth.

The waitress returns his smile. Christopher's eyes stay on the waitress as she walks away. Emma seems annoyed with the amount of attention Christopher pays the waitress. She takes a deep breath and lets out a loud exhale hoping to regain Christopher's undivided.

"You know, your good looks and my money won't carry you very far after you graduate. Your lack of motivation is starting to annoy me," she hastily puts her yellow pad and pen away in her messenger bag that's draped over her chair.

"Hey, I can always join the military."

She jumps in, "Over my dead and decaying corpse. I can't even handle the thought, let alone the reality of that. Don't even joke about it."

"Okay! But it's not my fault! I thought I was going to be a history teacher until last month when it occurred to me that history is history," he laughs at his own joke. Emma does not.

She looks directly at him. "I want to help you, but you need to figure some of this shit out on your own. What turns you on? I don't necessarily mean job related. During your whole day what sticks out most in your mind's eye? Visualize the things that you come across. Things that you see or hear or feel that you remember most."

"You sound like you're reading from a pamphlet," he laughs again, trying to keep things light.

"Shut it. I'm serious. What dreams did you have when you were a kid? Tell me. I don't care if they sound silly. And don't disappoint me that you don't have any. That won't fly. You're too much my brother not to have something in you that you absolutely need to accomplish," Emma tries not to sound as exasperated as she feels.

Christopher looks down at the menu on the table, "You hungry?"

"Are you listening?"

"Yeah."

168

"Are you hearing me? You want to fiddlefuck around or do you want to make something of yourself?"

"Look, I have that connection at the post office if that job with your friend doesn't work out. Ok?"

Emma shakes her head, "Oh my god. So is that it? I always have to come through for you? You do realize you're talking about a fallback job at nineteen." Emma points to a Mercedes parked at the corner, "You see that? You will never drive a new Mercedes as a civil servant. Find something you're willing to sweat blood for. I know you've got it in you, Christopher. I believe in you, always have. It's time you start believing in yourself."

Christopher looks down at his shoes, at a loss for words. Emma hates seeing him like this, hurts her heart to have to be so strict. But tough love is sometimes the only way to reach the unmotivated, a shove in any direction other than simply staring at one's own four-walled mind.

6. Down We Go

    Standing in front of the tall fridges in the deli attempting to decipher between Stella Artois and anything else, Trick grabbed two six-packs of the green beer and headed for the counter. The sun had come up several hours ago and she wasn't about to go home any time soon, to pace her apartment relentlessly alone. Matt came in to buy a lottery ticket, seducing a smile out of her, promising on good faith to split the earnings with her. She paid for the beer and then told him to carry the bags.

Several weeks ago was her birthday and she'd spent it alone in a movie theatre all day watching actors force portrayals of meaningful experiences, one after the next, and the whole thing made her cry because the falsity removed her further from the human condition. She was left feeling cold. In between screenings, she noticed a missed call on her cell phone from her Mom, but she imagined that it only came out of a kind of courtesy. She returned the call to repeat the annual slogan, "Thanks for giving birth to me", hoping to convey some semblance of joy through her staged grin. She figured the words would sound better if said through a stretched mouth. The fact was she hated birthdays. They reminded her of her own failings, with time running out to do anything about it. Her mother's voice did soothe her, however, as she represented the only real love she knew in this world, and it
170

brightened her spirits enough to want to go out and do something about her self loathing.

She set out to maneuver her way into a new crowd. She was tired of feeling defeated and alone all the time, and sought the good, available few to pique immediate interest, or what she liked to call "enthusiasm at the ready". There was much missing from the life of solitude she had willfully chosen after Jimmy, and she was not sure when she stopped liking the company she kept while alone. After her experience at Donnie's, she got to thinking about why she ran away. What was she afraid of? Fun? She had to assume that in order to stave off the loneliness she kept feeling, she would have to seek out the company of others. Maybe she would feel differently if she belonged to something. She hadn't yet figured out what she wanted to do with her life, so she wasn't sure where to begin, opting for a big dive in any one direction to see where it led.

The crew she attached herself to turned out to be vicious with no real means to advance, but with huge aspirations. They gave her some cocaine and instead of feeling vulnerable, she felt powerful and she forged ahead because they were beautiful to look at and free of structure, respecting each other the way friends were supposed to. For now, there were no thoughts of love and a happy home, nor was a career at the forefront. She was still young and having fun. She looked forward to losing herself in the madness of others, taking the drug socially whenever they all gathered. Fuck it, she told herself. There's nothing I've got to do tomorrow that's so goddamn important. With this new mindset, she bore witness to the sunrise more times each week than a person living with some semblance of order and responsibilities would ever see in a lifetime. Plus, it turned her on.

Her stomach ached as she shed weight. She danced in dark, red curtained clubs with others also suffering from definitive intoxication, presuming the stories they were making held quality, something of interest later. Everybody was chasing a high that amounted to nothing, she started secretly deducing, but that didn't stop her from playing. It wasn't that she expected to find a better way. She knew this was no way out of her state of disarray. But it passed the time in a unique way. People she'd met only once before would greet her like an old
172

friend, with hugs and kisses, where she lacked intimate contact otherwise. It wasn't bad, because it didn't feel bad. She had the energy of a jaguar and made herself feel beautiful by dressing the part every time she went out. Could she find something other than what she began to expect from these people? There was no question the men she met could hardly conduct themselves with dignity, so she felt safe from falling, again, in love. The prospect was not a very welcome venture. She couldn't trust men with her heart. That much she knew. Better to stay single, she had decided, but secretly knew that shutting oneself off from the possibility of anything would mean ultimate defeat. And that wasn't an option. She had to get out of the apartment as often as her will permitted to see what came next.

Matt opened the front door of his apartment and everybody filed in. There was stifled laughter, as a consideration for the neighbors, until it was realized that most of the people in the building had already left for work. Music erupted as some genius in the group figured out how to operate the sound system. Tony was on the phone with his dealer as girls lined up to await the pour of the rest of his cocaine on the huge, glass coffee table, cutting lines for everyone to participate in the perpetual continuation of the "good time". Trick sat on the couch and lit a cigarette. She attributed her newfound smoking habit to a temporary distraction from the craziness that seemed to constantly surround her. She hugged herself, feeling the effects of being out every night this week but Friday and Saturday. In the city, the weekends belonged to the Bridge and Tunnel crowd. It wasn't fun to share a dance floor with forty Guidos from Jersey. She had adapted to her new lifestyle by working weekends at a restaurant job she hated and enjoyed poking fun at anyone who didn't keep her unique party schedule. This included tourists, families, suits, and college students. It was hard to care about anyone but yourself and, of course, your friends. The search for an extended family, a place to belong, never ceased. She felt like a true New York City native, a gritty, dirty savage in an unforgiving, concrete jungle.

A desperately skinny girl wearing a black top hat approached Trick and rattled off confessions. "Hi, do we know each other? Anyway, it's my birthday and

174

I told my boyfriend I'm going all out. I don't care. I wanna have a good time."

"Are you succeeding?" Trick mused.

"In my career? Hardly. I can't stand the business. Full of too many assholes who just want to sleep with you and then you never get the part. I don't care. I'm thinking about going back to school. But I don't know. Maybe I'll settle down. But not with him," she pointed to the great looking guy who was mastering the positively appropriate music for the weary daylight. He was cute and seemed skilled, so Trick inquired what it was this hyperactive stick figure was looking for, then exercised her right to protect herself from other people's drama by only half listening and drawing heavily on her cigarette.

"Oh, I don't know, I mean, he's a great guy. But I can't have kids, you know? It's my kidneys. They wouldn't be able to take it. That's what the doctor says. So I think it's not fair, you know? I mean, he's such a great guy."

Tony could be heard making a toast to the birthday girl. She squealed and ran off to do the first line before all the other cokeheads, who were promising some sort of orgy as soon as the dealer got there. Trick watched the boyfriend view his fragile princess dipping headlong into the pile and saw him shake his head.

Matt came over and sat down with two beers, handing her one. He produced a clear packet of his own stash and she accepted without hesitation. She was already so awake, she wondered what another bump could possibly do for her. She remembered the deejay from the club the night before playing his farewell set that included all his best music. They had spent the night celebrating his stint at a short-lived hotspot. She vaguely remembered vomiting in a dark corner of the club as someone yelled, "It's not a party unless Trick vomits!" and everyone laughing at her shame. These thoughts ran through her diluted mind as she hovered over her house key to scrape the inside of the plastic bag to administer more of the substance into her body. She wiped at her nostril and handed him back the bag. "Hey, Matt. Are you having a good time?"

"Nowhere I'd rather be," he said, with a smug grin on his face.

"Really? Have you ever been anywhere outside the U.S.? I'm thinking there are so many things to see, you know? And I'm not

176

sure all this is so great," she sighed and took a swig from her beer bottle.

"Yeah, sure. I've been to Korea. And Germany. Australia's cool."

"Really? How long was the flight?" She was amazed this dude had been anywhere, even though he professed all sorts of talents. What he really seemed to excel at was wasting time.

"Long. But it's beautiful. You go anywhere and it opens your eyes. Serious. You think you can go your whole life and not see the world?" From across the room, Tony made some primal sound indicating that he had found another score tucked into his wallet when secretly she knew this was his signature move. He liked to surprise his audience with more to come, kept them guessing. She had seen him do this before and he was really good at it. The gesture seemed to get cheers from the crowd every time. Even Matt bounced over to the table to do a line. Trick got up and followed him because, she thought, what the hell else am I doing?

After she put the rolled up dollar bill to nose and snorted some "inspiration", she took a deep sip of her beer and walked out to the terrace to take in the view. She hadn't realized how high up they were. The elevator had taken a while, but from the time she had willingly thrown herself into this mix, she'd experienced trouble ascertaining the time. It had become irrelevant as she lived by a twenty-four clock. She stood out on the balcony looking at the sun in its position, positing it as being about nine o'clock. But then, who really knew for sure? None of these people wore watches.

"It's 9:38," a voice said, and she turned to meet it. His skin was freckled, his face held a big nose, and his body carried slim shoulders. He was somewhat handsome. She wanted everyone to be gorgeous and, at this hour, they best be.

"Super," she had left her beer somewhere and had nothing to toast the hour. He handed her his beer and she took some. "Thanks."

"Joel. I've seen you around. I guess we've never formally met." He stuck out his thin hand and she took it.

"Hi, Joel. I'm Trick. Not my real name, but whattya gonna do?" She laughed because she had said this many times before and somehow it always sounded fresh.

"What's your real name?" he took the bottle back and looked out onto the city below.

178

"Does it matter?"

"It should to you," he said, spitting off the side of the building. She decided it was just gross enough to join him. She gathered up her phlegm and jutted out her chin to reach beyond her scope. She had enough collected from the night to hock a substantial load through her nose and out of her mouth. It felt good.

"Oh, my goodness," she exclaimed.

"Not bad, for a priss."

"What'd you call me?"

"Don't get bent outta shape. I've seen you out. You seem to be saving yourself for something," he looked back through the glass sliding doors, uncomfortable.

"That's how well you know people," she turned away.

"What, I'm wrong? A beautiful girl like you? If you're not saving yourself for something, then I don't know what," he swigged the rest of the beer and headed inside.

"I used to be a prostitute," she blurted out. For whatever reason, her heart wanted to get this piece of news out of the way before her head could stop her.

He turned, stopping in place. "Bullshit."

"Bull true," she pulled out her cigarettes and gave him one when he immediately reached for them with his strange, skinny fingers. They looked as if they'd been broken at one point and that reminded her of Pam, and how they'd fallen out after her breakup with Jimmy. Pam still inadvertently blamed her for ruining a good thing. Trick was giving her time to get over it.

"Like, a dancer?" he shrugged.

"No, like a pro. A hooker. Sex for money. Surprised? I'm sure you are. But at this point in my life it doesn't matter what anybody thinks. They can all go fuck themselves."

"No shit. I've felt that way all my life. In high school I had no friends. Fuck the world and everybody in it. You do what you gotta do," he inhaled cigarette smoke. "I'm not judging you."

"I tried love once. And love sucks. Totally. I'd rather be alone. So, I am. You?" she spotted a blonde dude walking out with the same idea they had. She smiled at him innocently and said, "Hey, what a beautiful day, huh? Can you get us two beers? I paid for 'em."

"Sure, no problem," he said and disappeared inside.

Joel turned to her. "What was it like?"

"What, getting paid for it? Better than not getting paid for it."

"No, falling in love," he said.

"You've never been in love? What's wrong with you?"

"I told you. I went to a high school where Jews were not accepted. There's nothing more to tell. It was fucking miserable. I got myself to count on," he was growing anxious with the subject matter.

"Seems you got out okay."

"You know that play 'By the Skin Of Our Teeth'? William Soroyan, or some shit. Don't ask me how I know it. That was me. I moved to the city and made my own friends."

"So, these are your friends."

"Whatever it takes. How long you been here?" he asked.

"Long enough."

The blonde guy resurfaced and handed them two beers. Joel suggested they partake in another line before all the drugs were gone and she agreed with that game plan. As he held his arm out in an exaggerated gesture for her to step inside first, she saw for the first time the tattoos covering his forearms and remembered him from the boat. She gave him a surprised look, and smiled. "What," he said. "Yes, there are still gentlemen out there in the world!" They laughed.

Joel called her later that same day. She couldn't recall giving him her number, so he appeared resourceful enough. He wanted to invite her out. There was something likable about the guy. She hadn't been able to discern his lot in life, if he had a job or not. But he was steadfast and told it like it was. And he didn't judge her for her past. If she stayed home to avoid the trouble she suspected he might get her into, she feared turning her viability into something conclusively irrelevant. "Sleep is overrated" had become her new motto because the constant nag that there was more to be done never ceased to elude her periphery. She had the energy to make mistakes. The time to do this shit was now, she thought. Through her newly gained perpetual hangover, Trick told him she'd love to and hung up the phone.

Later that night, she met him in front of a hot club that seemed to have everyone in town trying to get in. Joel grabbed her hand and pushed his way right to the front. The bouncers recognized him immediately, opened the red velvet rope, and they walked right in. She was impressed. The darkened atmosphere was ripe for more dancing and drugging. Trick took a deep, informed breath. She was about to fly high again and that made her smile, but a tiny voice deep inside her mind blew a kiss of doubt. She squashed it immediately. Where were we all really going in the end? She laughed at the attempt at digging into the abyss of the larger questions beyond her scope at the present moment. Leave it alone! She cried. You're here now! So what of tomorrow? Moments passed by each day, losing traction to the moments that replaced them, as the next replaced the next. The carefree mood she felt right now provided a cheerful stage with which to act out her existential play on living in the present. She picked up her pace and caught up to Joel without further hesitation.

They worked their way to the corner banquet, as Joel was greeted by lots of people who seem to know him. She immediately recognized the player from Montreal she saw dancing on the boat, who threw his hips around on top of the banquet as he reached out a hand for her to climb up through the swaying bodies to dance with him. They moved well together and he kissed her when she didn't expect it and it was a good kiss. She recognized him as the true player he was, wearing his lifestyle on his sleeve for everyone to see. He was the type to subsist on free rides. Amidst the loud music, that little voice in her head became louder, reminding her of who she wanted to become, admitting to herself through the noise that she ought to seek familial investments, friends and eventual lovers with staying power. Dancing with him while everyone watched caused a sense of starry-eyed perfection, the club goers approving of their sexy ways, but there would be an end to it before it even had a chance to begin. This was a mere vague connection thru the induced haze that would most certainly result in sex funk aftermath for him with someone not her, as she was not interested in anything casual with a player. There was no blaming him. She just knew better and opted instead to excuse herself and headed for the bathroom. As she made her way down one of the many dark pathways, she spotted a back room and investigated.

She had lost sight of him in the ever-morphing crowd, but there he now sat with his core group. Joel held court and

184

looked more beautiful than she remembered from the boat, or, for that matter, this morning on the terrace of the dehydrating living dead, and she wanted to snuggle close to his confidence. He saw her approaching from far off and held back no surprise as he welcomed her, as if his wish had been granted. She had found him on her own in all the chaos and he celebrated her for it. She liked his enthusiasm. He was a man who had obviously endured this scene for a long time yet continued his search for the one beauty that insisted on safety through her foraging in the land of the hedonists, that continued to terrify parents and concerned teachers who had done all they could to guide their kids toward responsible positions in society, to unite with him as an eventual better half. Yet, in their short conversation on this precarious morning, Trick wasn't altogether convinced Joel hadn't been relegated as some sort of minion of evil. He followed his drive to drink and drug every day of his unemployable life. He was ruthless and called it righteousness. His tone attacked and his demeanor apologized for nothing. But he had been one of the five to dance on deck in the rain and looked at her as if she were the only woman alive and she felt the overwhelming need to ignite something, against her stance on love. She knew he was a catch in this scene because he refused everyone and because he was showing certain interest in her, she felt special. She sat down next to him with a bit of earned arrogance. He offered her a bump and, in the bottom recesses of who her grown up self was becoming, she knew that she was sitting next to a man that pulled no punches. She warned herself now and forever more, there was always going to be contention with this guy. He was loud and obnoxious and always had to have the floor. He was the type to talk over people and he always did whatever the fuck he wanted. Tread carefully.

Whatever, she said to herself. I'm on loan right now anyway. I accept it. She dove into the conversation with an attractive demeanor, directing her efforts primarily towards Joel. She had a lot to say and needed an audience. She felt beautiful and on fire. The cocaine helped.

"Oh, you say whatever you want," a heavyset, dyed-blonde Russian girl with bad teeth interjected.

186

"Why not? Why else would you leave the house?" Trick laughed, taking Joel's glass and drinking, starting to feel everything at once.

"Your girl's got a mind of her own," the fat crazy Russian said.

"I'm wondering what else you think there is," Trick positioned her face in line with this powerhouse you either put up or shut up to.

"Baby, I got nothing to prove to you," the Russian wasn't taking any crap.

"Yeah you do. I just met you. How do you want to be considered?"

"Like I give a shit. You aren't nothing but a thing. Joel will fuck you and forget you."

"Whoa," Joel interjected, not ready to have his cover blown by some loose cannon.

"Really? And you call each other friends? Fine, let's all cut each other down before we have a chance to shine," Trick thought she had nothing to lose and nearly went for the fat Russian's throat.

"Joel, you got a live one on your hands," the heavyset girl said.

"Kira, I like this girl. Yo, why don't you shut the fuck up?" Joel admitted, holding Trick back in a flirtatious way.

"It's your life, baby. All I'm sayin', you got a big problem on your hands. You deal with it," Kira looked off towards the dancing masses.

"Thanks for the compliment. Coming from you, that should mean something." Trick sneered.

"It's my deal, Kira, ok?" Joel took a drink. Trick tempered herself, readying to fly off at any moment. Joel saw it and it turned him on. He said to the Russian, "You wish you were me right now. I know you want to take this girl home. There's no fucking way I'm letting her go. You understand?" He locked eyes with the woman and she backed down, realizing she didn't stand a chance because something else was happening here.

"You know it's good when you see it, baby. You are good and I love it," the Russian laughed wickedly and removed her big body from the table. Trick and Joel and the rest of the onlookers watched her go. This was a certain battle won.

Trick thought, I will follow this man as long as it takes to find truth and justice, or until the drugs become too much, which already they were. Once a junkie (cheater, liar, thief), always a junkie, her mom taught her that, but
188

whatever. Who wants their life lessons handed to them right away?

Emma, wearing an ill-fitted dress and strangled by a crocheted black scarf, sits uncomfortably at the bar of a local watering hole while Teresa, slowly nursing a soda, jaws passionately about her drug-fueled days with something resembling glee. Emma's yellow legal pad is on the bar but she isn't taking any notes. She rests her chin on her hands, eyes closed, and listens. She opens them in order to thumb down the bartender for another drink, gagging down the one in front of her in one gulp. She stares ahead as Teresa yammers on. Emma grows weary and sighs, wasted youth gnawing at her insides. She had spent her teenage years raising Christopher and subsequently toiled away at her first book thereafter. She knows she must not judge this young woman. There is a story here. Stick with it. Don't give up, she begs of herself. Still, she hates this lack of direction. She expects more from others, not unlike Trick. The thought makes Emma smirk.

There she sat. Her insides felt like shit. Her skin crawled. She tried to remember a time when she felt good above all else and couldn't. It seemed everything sucked and she was sad for lack of love and understanding. It will pass, she whispered, but didn't believe even herself anymore.

Joel was putting her through paces and he wasn't even able to help himself. He conducted lessons in righteousness every day, but left her wondering what she was fighting for. What was he even talking about? It all seemed so strange to Trick because she never doubted her own integrity, even when she had hustled strangers for money. She always felt as if she were duly earning her dollars because she'd always been straight up. And now, every night that she wasn't working the door at some nightclub for a lousy hundred bucks, she'd be out with Joel and Tony and Gigi and Eddie and any other straggler that would collect like lint on a wool suit. But if there was a confrontation resulting in some sort of altercation on the basis of standing one's ground, she felt forced to move away from what was really happening and take cover under the pretense that the other was always right, otherwise she would get a fist in her face, the part of her that respected herself long ago lost in the search for communion. Forgetting what was real, the ride moved forward and she had paid her fare, taken her seat, and now waited for something real to feel. Whether fear or acceptance, the drugs kept her close enough to still suspect answers were on their way. Do enough of one thing and something's bound to come out of it, she remembered hearing someone say, she just wasn't sure who said it or why and wished for something to happen soon. At the end of long night out, it only made sense to stop all the nonsense, pull out and make something good with her life. The hangover refused to subside and the answers were still nowhere in sight. Back to the bar for another round.

The last time she and Joel fought, the cops were called and she found herself excusing his actions. No, officer, I don't want to press charges, she heard herself saying, because she knew that would put an end to everyone's fun. Besides, she hadn't gotten hurt. She and Joel had started sleeping together. It was inevitable because he had openly fallen in love with her for all their friends to see and he was the type of guy that didn't shut the fuck up until he got what he wanted. She liked denying his sexual advances initially, secretly admitting to herself that she was above committing to this madman who had no control over his temper. Yet getting his brand of golden attention made her feel adored, an adventure always around the corner. So she gave in.

"I love you," he'd say.

"Good. Thank you." Her inconclusiveness was comfortable. She was on borrowed time because she still had a lot of figuring out left to do. This wasn't real, she whispered to herself in her darkest moments. Deep down, she stayed strong for her.

Chapter 7

The gym is busy for this time of day. Emma wears loose running pants and a sweatshirt. She holds a towel in one hand, headphones and a bottle of water in the other. She approaches a Stairmaster and prepares herself for a workout. She struggles with untangling the headphones and drops the towel. She retrieves it, trying to place it over the numbers on the machine to prevent herself from watching the clock. She balances the bottle of water in the cup holder, climbing on the machine and punching in the settings. She straightens the towel once more and goes through the motions for several minutes before holding her abdomen in pain and climbs off. She gathers her things, frustrated, and walks off.

The restaurant is darkly lit and nearly empty, as patrons leave with smiles and light conversation. Emma sits at a table alone. There is a tall glass half full of whiskey and ice in front of her. She reads from a magazine as the waiter drops off the check. Without looking up, she places her credit card on top of the bill and continues to read the article.

She holds her coat over one arm, moving through the restaurant, passing the bar. She grimaces, holding her stomach in pain. As she is putting on her coat, she hears the sexy voice of a woman talking loudly at the bar.

"You have to live your life the way you want to be. I'm fighting for my right to smoke. Like my ex-girlfriend fights for her right to not wear a helmet when she rides.

Sure, when she's in town she wears it. But she tells me when she's on an open road, it should be her choice whether or not to wear a helmet. Am I right?"

Emma turns to see a beautiful brunette talking to the bartender. When Emma stops to stare at the woman, she turns to stare back. She has deep, dark eyes lined with heavy black eyeliner. She wears a sexy, slinky black dress that reveals five pounds of tit in a one-pound bag.

"Hello," she purrs.

"Hi," Emma responds awkwardly.

"Want to stay? Have a drink?"

Emma pauses, considering the invitation. She grabs at her abdomen, briefly, and decides to stay, "Sure. Why not?" She moves to the bar and takes a seat next to the woman.

"Barbara," she says, offering her a beautifully manicured hand.

"Emma. How do you do?"

"Oh, I'm good, honey. Just bitching."

"Understood."

"What's your bad self up to?"

"I'm a writer."

194

"Oh goody! What are you writing?" Barbara rubs her legs together.

"I don't know. A story about a misguided young woman. I think I've written her into a corner."

"Well, what do you want to say? The young are as interesting as my ovaries. I care about them, but how much time can I spend thinking about them, really? It will all figure itself out."

Emma smiles at this beauty. She turns to the bartender. "Can I get a Maker's Mark on the rocks?"

The bartender nods.

Emma turns to Barbara. "Can I buy you a drink?"

"Honey, your drink's on me. Stan, give me a Cosmo."

The Bartender busies himself with their drinks. Barbara turns towards Emma and gently touches her arm. "I appreciate so much when people can create. I'm a bartender and half the time, I don't know where the fuck it will lead. But one thing I know for sure? I care about my happiness more than most. And in that, I treat others with the kindness I want to be treated with."

Emma nods imperceptibly. "I don't get out much," she realizes how that sounds and looks down.

"Honey, what's wrong? You look stressed."

"Stop calling me honey. I'm not your honey."

"You could be. I think you're beautiful. In fact, your beauty hits hard."

"Oh, my."

"What? It doesn't?"

Emma waves a hand. "Please don't. I don't know how to take a compliment anymore. Only criticism has found its way to me as of late."

The drinks arrive and Emma takes a large gulp. As she swallows, she looks away. Barbara doesn't. She grabs her arm again.

"You need to stop being such a bad self and start being your bad self. I'm serious! Why hold back? You're being way too hard on yourself."

"I have a personal deadline," Emma says, deadpan.

"Ooh, that sounds serious," Barbara laughs loudly. "Come on, honey. We all do. But you've got to live first! Why don't you come home with me?"

Emma laughs. When she stops laughing, she says, "What?"

"I want you to see where I live. Hang out with me. It won't kill you to see how the other half lives. When was the last time you spent the night at someone else's house? We'll have a sleep over! Loosen you up. Give ya something to write about."

"You have no idea," Emma snickers. "Sorry, I... I can't."

"I'm just telling you what I see. If you don't like me, that's fine. I like myself enough for the both of us. But something tells me you could stand for some fun. When was the last time you had any fun?" Barbara throws her hands in the air. "Live a little!"

Emma finally meets her eyes. "I don't dance on command. Why are you pushing me?"

Barbara leans in closer to meet her gaze head on. "Look, I'm a fighter for my rights, same as you. I see you," she pauses, looking for the right words. "I hate the word 'no' so much because it stops the natural progression of things. I'm not a writer, but I'm all about my stories. Without them, we are nothing but useless bags of fear. That's not the life I want to live. Come have a good time with me. It'll do wonders for your health. Seriously, where are we without our experiences?"

Emma follows Barbara inside her warm apartment with an overpowering Asian motif. There are Tibetan Buddha statues and candles scattered everywhere that Barbara begins lighting. The smell of Nag Champa permeates the air. Emma takes off her coat and makes herself comfortable on the couch. Barbara grabs a bottle of white wine from the kitchen and two glasses.

"I just love white wine. My beautiful gay friend calls it desperate and trashy. Don't you just love that! And don't you just love my place? I got this apartment eight years ago for such an awesome deal, there's just no moving out." Barbara anxiously joins Emma on the couch and pours the wine, handing her a glass. "Here. Cheers!"

They toast, then drink. There's an awkward silence. Emma looks around the room. Barbara takes the glass from her and sets both on the table. She advances on Emma, kissing her. Emma responds with uncertainty. Barbara continues to kiss her softly, until something takes over Emma and she grabs Barbara by the hair, causing her to moan. They begin taking each other's clothes off, kissing continuously and groping each other in a blur of the heat of the movement. Emma is tearing into her with real zeal. Barbara suddenly stops them.

"Hold on, okay? I want to show you something. I'll be right back. Don't you move," she untangles herself from Emma, who is left half undressed and holding her head, shaking it in confusion. She tries to stand and is gripped by the pain in her abdomen. She clutches her stomach, looks down at herself half dressed, and gathers her clothing that has twisted itself around her legs and arms. Before she can compose herself completely, Barbara returns with a strap on, black dildo fastened to her half-naked body. "Look at my new toy!" she says, standing above Emma, who stares. "I hope it's not too intimidating? Let's give it a shot. Have you ever used one before?"

198

Emma begins to laugh uncontrollably, stopping to hold her stomach in pain. "No. I don't think so. I don't feel very well."

Barbara sits next to her. "Oh, honey. What's wrong?" Barbara looks at her sweetly, the dildo standing at attention between her legs.

Emma continues to clutch her stomach, "I don't know. I think it's my stomach."

"Food poisoning?" Barbara asks with genuine concern.

"No. I don't know. I'd better go. I'm sorry."

"Do you want me to take you to the hospital?"

"No, I loathe hospitals. I'll be alright," she says unconvincingly and tries to stand up straight. She leaves Barbara on the couch, looking confused and dejected, clutching the dildo in one hand.

Emma sits on her toilet, consumed with worry. She wipes herself, looking at the paper and finds it covered with blood. She looks into the bowl. The toilet water is red. She moves to the bed to rest, but sleep seems an impossible task as a garbage truck outside her window clangs metal onto metal, the sound echoing through her loft and traveling right through her brain. She curls up into a ball in extreme angst.

It is not a good morning. Emma picks up the phone and dials.

Christopher is cooking scrambled eggs and green peppers while talking on the phone to his girlfriend of the week. The phone beeps, indicating an incoming call. "Hold on, Maria. I got another call, ok?" he switches to the incoming call. "Hello?"

"Hey."

"Hey, sis. Can you hold on? Stay with me."

"Sure."

He switches back, "I gotta take this."

Maria is immediately pissed and starts yelling, "You know I'm not gonna teach you how to dance so you can dance with some other bitch!"

"Stop. Will you? It's my sister. I'll call you later."

"Your sister always comes first, maricon. Bendejo!" Maria screams into the phone.

He ignores her and quickly switches back, pouring the eggs onto a plate and setting himself up at the small kitchen table to eat. "How's the writing going?"

"Slow. How are you?"

"Didn't you hear? I'm changing majors. Business/Finance."

200

Emma sits on the couch in a ball, clutching the phone to her face. She whispers, "You know that I'm proud of you, right?"

"But I haven't done anything yet."

"It's all right. You've done all the right things by me all this time. I wish I would've found someone like you along the way," she whispers lethargically.

Christopher puts his fork down. "Sis, are you all right? You don't sound good. Do you need me to come in?

Emma 's voice becomes even lower. "I'm in a lot of pain, actually."

"I'll be there by eight."

"Okay. Thank you, Christopher. Loveyoubye."

"Loveyoubye."

Emma struggles to get up, drags her feet as she walks over to the kitchen and opens the refrigerator. She looks inside. It's full of condiments and nothing else. She quickly closes the fridge door and starts to undress. She goes into the bathroom, turns on the shower and stops in front of the full-length mirror. She stares at herself through frightened eyes. Her belly is distended, her eyes sunken in, dark circles around them. She's a mess and she's finally noticing it.

Christopher pulls up to his friend Ron's house in his red Jeep Cherokee. He goes around back and descends the staircase to the basement. There are two guys playing pool with Ron, who is half Asian, half Caucasian. He greets Christopher animatedly, smiling and goofing off. "Pool shark's here! We're in trouble, now! Hey Chango, you here to take all our money, ese?"

Christopher smiles. "I'll spare you, Ron, if you hold my chalk."

"Get Christopher a beer!" Ron shouts.

"No, Dude I can't stay. I'm going into the city."

"Alright, man. When we leavin'?"

One of Ron's friends says, "We can't. We're meeting up with those girls from the Shagwong."

"Dude, you'd rather meet Shag hags then go into the city?"

"I'd rather drive 10 miles for a sure thing then a hundred miles, blow a buck fifty on lap dances and take turns jerking off in the back seat on the drive home."

The second guy chimes in, "As long as you don't make any noise! Don't be gruntin'!" They all laugh and give each other high fives.

Ron looks at Christopher. "Alright, Dude. It's me and you."

202

"No really, Ron. My sister is having a rough time, I think. I'm going to go see her by myself tonight. For dinner, or something."

"Fuck off, Dude. Why can't I go with you? She laughs at me all the time. Maybe that's just what she needs tonight. A dose of Ron the idiot."

"I don't know. I'll call her and see if it's alright first."

"Of course it is. She loves me."

Christopher walks to another part of the room and calls Emma. He gets the answering machine.

Emma is in the shower letting the water wash over her face. Her phone rings. Christopher's voice is heard on the machine. "You there? I wanted to ask you if Ron could join us. He's at least good for a laugh. Well... Um... Call me soon so I can let him know. Call me, call me, call me back! Where you at? Hello? Olly Olly Oxen free! Tag, you're it! Loveyoubye," he hangs up.

Emma gets out of the shower, wraps herself in a towel and walks into her closet.

The guys are playing another game of pool. Christopher pockets his cell phone. He pulls Ron aside. "Ron, you know what? I'm going to go by myself. I think it's best."

"Dude, fuck that. Don't make me tie myself to the bottom of your truck. How about this? I'll even drive."

"Alright, fine. Let's go. Get ready. Wear something nice."

"Come on! Who dresses better than me?"

"Uh, me. Matter of fact, everybody, dude."

"Fuck you. Let me get my hat and I'll be down in a minute. Don't leave!"

Christopher sits in the passenger side of Ron's beat up 1980 Hyundai Elantra. Ron is sifting through radio stations. "Dude, guess who I saw yesterday. Sadie. Is it time, yet? Can I go after her now? Can I have her? Can I finally make her mine?"

"What did I tell you about that? Quit fucking around."

"She's never had half Asian yet. You know what they say, once you go half Asian..."

Christopher is concerned and frustrated, watching the road.

Ron persists, "C'mon, man. When are you going to lighten up? You've got your señorita. What's up with her?"

"Ron, did anyone ever tell you you're delusional? And in need of professional help? Medication perhaps?"

"Oh, my brother, medication is my specialty. I thought you knew that by now. Must I remind you who was the one that showed you the power of alcohol and it's magical affects on the ladies."

Christopher focuses on the breaking traffic ahead. He sees what, in the evening dusk, appears to be a tire bouncing in the road towards the concrete divider. The tire is approaching rapidly and leaps the divider heading right towards Ron's car. "Look out, Ron!"

Ron turns to see the oncoming tire as it crashes through their windshield. Ron loses control of the car, veering into the concrete divider causing the car to flip over and skid into the middle of the highway where it is struck by two oncoming cars behind them. All of the traffic comes to a halt on both sides of the highway.

Ron stirs as people are standing around the car. An elderly man speaks directly at Ron. "Are you okay? Son, are you hurt?"

Ron looks around and realizes he is upside-down, blood dripping into both of his eyes making it difficult for him to see.

A stocky woman stands above him, "I'm a nurse. Don't move. What's your name? Do you know where you are?" Ron is unable to respond. She yells to the crowd that has formed. "Has someone called an ambulance? Somebody get an ambulance! Does anyone have a phone?"

Ron looks sideways towards Christopher and does not see his head. Blood is everywhere. Ron is confused and starts to shake uncontrollably.

Bystanders are hovering over the wreck, gaping. A young man screams out, "SOMEONE GET A BLANKET! DOES ANYONE HAVE ANYTHING TO COVER UP THIS GUY?"

The nurse wipes Ron's face as he begins to cry, trying desperately to find Christopher in the wreckage. The nurse holds Ron's face to prevent him from looking as the young man does his best to cover Christopher's headless body with a blanket.

Emma checks the clock. It's almost 9:00. She grabs a cigarette and lights it. She takes a long hard drag and goes back to the bathroom. She stands in front of the mirror and brushes her hair. She comes out of the bathroom and calls Christopher's cell phone. It goes straight to voicemail. "Hey, Where are you? Are you stuck in traffic? Call me," she grows frustrated, adding, "I'm starting to finally get hungry. Imagine that." She hangs up the phone and walks back into her closet and starts looking for something else to wear. She removes the shirt she was wearing, hanging it back up. She grabs another shirt off a hanger and walks back into the bathroom with it.

Emma returns from the bathroom and the red flashing light from the answering machine finally catches her eye. She walks over to it and her hands start to shake as she pushes the play button. Christopher's message

206

plays. "... Where you at? Hello? Olly Olly Oxen free! Tag, you're it! Loveyoubye."

Emma calls Christopher's cell phone again. The call goes straight to voicemail again. She hangs up the phone. She walks back into the living room and sits on the couch and starts to bite at her nails. She pulls out a magazine and flips through it with no interest.

A short time later, Emma checks the time, her answering machine, and then her cell phone. She dials Christopher's cell phone, "Hey, where the fuck are you? You're an hour and a half late. Please give me a quality excuse this time. I don't ask for much." Emma hangs up and dials Christopher's apartment phone number. The answering machine comes on and Emma hangs up. She goes over to the bar and pours herself a large whiskey.

Emma's phone rings. She races to pick it up, "Hello?" Emma hears crying on the other end of the line. "Hello!"

"Emma?" More crying.

"Mom?" Emma hears her mother crying. "Christopher?" she croaks. The crying grows louder and more intense. Emma screams. Her hand with the phone slowly falls from her face. The phone is dropped on the floor. "No!!!" Emma falls to the floor in a half seated position and pulls at her hair. Her body slumps.

Emma is in an emergency room bed with a cotton gown on, an IV attached to her arm. She is staring forward, blankly, devoid of any feeling. The stale air and fluorescent lighting cover her body like a shroud. A doctor comes in and takes the seat next to her.

"Ms. Montgomery, I understand you just suffered a tremendous loss. But I need to ask you again. How much have you been drinking?" The doctor's brows are furrowed, his eyes on the paperwork attached to his clipboard.

There's a deep silence. Emma turns to meet the doctor's concerned gaze, numb. She answers flatly, "How much you got?"

The sun is fading on another day. Rush hour traffic is merciless. A cab pulls up and James helps Emma out of the cab and into the building.

Emma is lying in her bed. The sheets are balled up around her. All the curtains in the loft are drawn closed which creates an almost totally dark room. James sits on the bed with her. She is curled up into a fetal position. He reaches out to her.

"I'm so sorry, Emma," he looks down at her face. "What do you need right now? Can I do anything?" Emma is catatonic. "You're not alone. I'm here now. I'll take care of everything."

She mutters to no one, "He can't be gone."

"I know. It's... It's unbelievable. I'm so sorry," he says.

Emma whispers, "He didn't even know who he was yet."

"It's okay, Em. He's supposed to be here with you, like this. There's a reason for everything."

"What's that supposed to mean?" Emma's voice rises.

"We don't know that now. Missing sometimes becomes the engine to move on. To survive."

"That's some bullshit."

"Sure. But that's the only thing I can think to say right now. Even priests I know. Everyone. There's no one way to say it. It's all placation for the really shitty situation that is death."

"Wow. That makes me feel better."

"The only way to explain it is that it happened for a reason. You want to get through this, don't you? Yeah, he was taken for a reason. I believe that. Trust me, it sounds like bullshit to me, too. I'm not totally convinced. But I have to believe in something. And so do you. Otherwise, this life is fucked."

Emma doesn't respond. His words echo in the room like a dull thud.

It is early morning. James is cooking something in the kitchen. Emma shifts in bed, uncomfortably. "I know you like your eggs over easy, but is scrambled okay? I really screwed the pooch with these guys," James shoots a look in her direction. A long silence follows. He carries over a plate of food to the bed. Emma remains motionless.

Emma is asleep. The loft is spotless. James is sitting at Emma's desk, working on his laptop. Emma wakes and walks to the couch wrapped in a blanket. She sits, staring ahead.

"I heard you mumbling in your sleep. Something about me being the best lover you've ever had," James softly laughs at his own joke.

Emma responds blankly, "Are you sure you weren't dreaming?"

James stands and moves over to the couch, "I was going to curl up next to you but I stood watch to make sure the boogey man stayed under the bed," he says, sitting.

"Thank you," she says flatly.

"Your neighbor is a freak, by the way. He watches TV in his underwear and takes two stuffed animal dogs and props them up on his hairy legs. Then he moves them up and down so they look like they're talking to one another. What a lonely guy." Emma doesn't respond. James continues, "Emma, how about I delay the release

210

of the book for awhile? We'll shoot for a fall release if you..."

"No. Why would you suggest that?"

James takes a minute before responding. "I just want to ease some of the pressure off you. It will be there when you're ready. No rush."

"Don't bring up work right now. I'm enjoying the pleasure of your company too much."

"Okay. Just want to make things easier," he stares at her slumped body. "How about a drink?" James walks over to the bar and pours two tall glasses of whiskey.

Emma says under her breath, "Yeah, just what the doctor ordered."

He brings the glasses to the couch. "To dying young and staying pretty. Here's to Christopher, for beating us to it."

Emma raises her glass, holding back her tears. They drink. He moves in to kiss her. She is numb, responding on autopilot.

Emma and James are moving together with familiarity. The sex is slow and methodical. He dominates and she acquiesces. They climax together loudly, releasing pent up tension. There is a period of calm, however brief, before James starts talking. He is animated.

"That was great. I'm so glad we did that. I've been looking forward to it all day. I couldn't wait for you to wake up."

She rolls on her side, away from him.

"Your pussy feels so good. Ah, man. I miss it. Let's go out. You wanna go get a drink?"

"James? Oh, James..." Emma sighs heavily.

"What?"

"Right, okay. Well, thanks."

"What do you mean?"

"Oh my God."

"What?"

"Get out."

"How about I make us some tea?"

"No. Too late for that. I want you to leave," she says matter-of-factly.

He moves to the kitchen and puts on water. He says flatly, "I'm not leaving you here alone."

Emma responds in monotone, "I want to be alone."

212

"The only time a writer wants to be alone is when they're experiencing true success. When the writing flows. They're sure of themselves again. I didn't start my job yesterday, you know."

"Fuck you."

"You expect too much from people. Why do you have to be so hard? You're not some character in your damn book, Emma! Why do you constantly feel the need to crush those closest to you?"

"Weeds out the weak."

"What's weak to you, huh? People who don't meet your expectations? You have some nerve! After all I've done for you!"

"James, I really don't think you know what's best for me, or else your cum wouldn't be dripping down my leg right now," she replies coldly.

"Okay, Emma. Maybe you're right. I have no idea how to handle this situation, clearly. But I do know what's best for me. I think it's time I go. I'll see you in the morning," James gathers his things and leaves.

Emma gets up, goes over to the refrigerator, and opens the door. She stands naked, staring. There are containers of leftovers from a delivery James ordered from the night before. She grabs the nearest metal bowl and crunches the plastic lid off in one motion. She picks up strands of cold, coagulated fettuccine with one hand and stuffs them into her mouth. She chews, continuing to fill her mouth with big, sloppy bites. She stares forward into nothingness as she chews, oil dripping down her chin and onto her bare breasts.

7. No Way Out

"Let's go dancing after this," Joel shouted over the music, grabbing at her tit with one hand, working the set of turntables in front of him with the other.

Trick was restless. She had only agreed to come out tonight for the free meal and drinks the owner provided for the dj. Money was tight for both of them and Joel was picking up random gigs to pay for their drugs. The place was filled with the kind of people they made fun of, the bridge and tunnel types, giving the already tacky place the feel of transience. It was common knowledge that these types of places came and went because they lacked the sophistication to draw a cooler clientele, one that would return because the spot had became a semi-permanent staple for them to spend their dollars.

She remained huddled in the dj booth, apart from the crowd, drinking herself into a stupor, while Joel was finishing up his set high on the coke Ricardo had delivered about two hours ago. Joel always needed blow to get through these gigs. In turn, he generously shoveled bumps up Trick's nose to keep her interested enough to endure the same songs he played night after night. She knew what he was doing to keep her there and it was okay. She was really the one in control, she told herself. I got this. Plus, there was nowhere else to go.

"I got somewhere we can go after this," he said, as if reading her mind. With him, there was always some new place to go, she smirked to herself, as she watched him busy himself with a big, black suitcase full of discs, old school style. When he tooled around Manhattan with that thing, it looked as if he were perpetually going on vacation. He put into the deck a disc of a mix he had cut earlier, packed up his things, and they took off into the night, leaving the crowd of drunken Jersey types to dance badly until they gained self-awareness that it was time to go home to their miserable lives. Joel's set wasn't officially over yet, but the disc he put on would hold them over for the duration. He liked cutting corners because it was his way of saying, "fuck you" to a job he felt a trained monkey could perform.

Their friend Gigi was a blonde, buxom beauty who knew how to drum up serious fun. She claimed aspirations for movie stardom. Now, in her thirties, she had never acted in anything, unless you call hustling her sex appeal for drugs performing. Trick certainly did, thinking Gigi was a natural and held nothing against her. In fact, she had an affinity for her style, her mysterious allure yet innocent demeanor. Appearing calm and clean and having that just-worked-out-at-the-gym glow, it didn't take long for her to get dirty. When she called, one only assumed the party was on because that sexy pussycat act was hard not to follow.

They responded in turn by getting into a cab and heading to the apartment of a personal trainer called Brad. Gigi enjoyed flirting with him at the gym and now he was inviting her and her friends over because a client of his was making an appearance and the client was a total nut case super hero something-or-other and always had more drugs than anyone had ever seen at any one time, according to Brad.

216

The door opened. "Hey, how's it going?" Brad greeted them with a warm smile. He was big and strong, as personal trainers go, and had manners that exceeded his stunning physique. A quiet, well-tempered man, he made them feel welcome in his modest apartment. They followed him into a small living room, taking seats on the black, leather loveseat as he poured out a significant amount of blow on the coffee tabletop.

Joel turned to Trick. "You ok?" he said, grabbing her hand and shaking it.

"Sure," she sighed and momentarily rested her head on his shoulder.

Gigi came out of the bathroom looking dewy and luscious, as usual, but her big, blue eyes carried insecurity. When Brad left the room to get something to cut the coke with, she whispered, "I really miss you guys."

"We miss you too, sweetheart," Joel said, grabbing her face and kissing it. Then, forever impatient, he dipped into the pile of coke in front of him using a fingernail. After a quick toot in one nostril, he said, "Where's Eddie?"

"He's on his way here," she smiled sweetly, yet slightly on edge.

Eddie and Gigi had designs on getting married as long as Trick knew them. She was mystified by the possibility of such a union succeeding because of how much uncertainty surrounding the duo. They seemed to find a precarious situation everywhere they went, with too many indiscretions and distractions coupled with an inherent procrastination to make and save any real money. Eddie went on the road a lot with his band while Gigi was a part-time massage therapist with her own brand of "specialties", making their future, as a happily married couple, seem anything but feasible. It was nice to see two people connect in a "we're in this together" sort of way, but could it really last?

When Eddie finally showed up, Gigi was visibly happier and more at ease, leaving Trick to presume that this is what it means to be in love despite the odds. She thought about Jimmy and how he made her feel when they first met and almost threw up from the loss.

They were well underway to chasing their high when Brad's client arrived. Bill Black was older and wore shorts and a muscle tee to show off his extreme fitness. He bounced around like a true force. He presented a large zip lock baggie filled with hundreds of ecstasy

218

pills, substantiating the rumor of having more drugs than she'd ever seen one person carry. He talked incessantly and carried a glass pipe around with him wherever he went, which he proceeded to smoke crystal meth out of throughout his entire diatribe of working as an advisor for top government officials. The whole thing seemed ludicrous, as they toasted the taking of the pills with a swig of straight vodka Brad had brought in from the kitchen. They stayed seated on the leather loveseat until the drug kicked in, making Trick's stomach clench. She reached for some tortilla chips on the table as fast as she could, hoping to counter the effects of severe nausea.

Bill decided it was time to relocate. Joel helped Trick up off the loveseat and down the stairs, as mere walking seemed challenging at this point. Everyone's voices became so much chatter. Trick couldn't connect with any one thing anyone was saying but held fast to the knowledge that she was only feeling this twisted because the drug was so powerful and to ride out this wave of nausea would mean hours of feeling the best she could ever feel. It was worth the minutes of bone racking torture to get to the other side. Still, she could barely trudge down those endless stairs without wanting to cry out in delirium and pain.

Bill was gay and that became quite clear after they arrived at his huge apartment. Once inside the safety of his own home, he transformed into a diva hostess, flirting with all the arriving men and producing even more provisions to a nearly saturated crowd. The brief tour of the expensive digs provided proof the guy hadn't been exaggerating. There was an entire room dedicated to framed photographs that blanketed the walls of Bill Black with every president since Carter, and not just shaking hands and smiling for the camera, either. No, these pictures gave way to intimate sessions that ranged from small park benches to the oval office itself, their new friend Bill "advising" the leaders of a nation that now seemed in full-blown trouble. Trick and Joel gazed upon these images, mouths agape. There was nothing left to do but remain respectful guests, simply laugh at life, and dance.

The movement helped her stomach considerably by pushing the drug out of her stomach, into her limbs and out to her fingertips. However, she needed to take the occasional break to regain balance, collapsing on an enormous chaise lounge chair and looking out of the large windows to behold the best views of the city she had ever seen. The Empire State Building dominated the landscape, its close proximity was dizzying. Bill's the real deal, she thought, as the music pumped through the posh surroundings. As more people arrived, friendly faces would make appearances throughout her drug haze with beautiful smiles and soft words. In fact, the good feeling prevailed for everyone, except for Bill. He was all business.

"Ok, everyone! Time for G shots! To the kitchen! Now!" he commanded the maniacal request dictatorially, in full voice.

"What did he say?" Trick said through a blur of movement, realizing her head hadn't stopped moving to the music and she had to tell herself to stop for a second to regain some composure and circumvent the vertigo.

"G. Have you ever done it before?" Joel asked lovingly, kissing Trick's hair and fingers.

"No. You?" she was so smiley.

"Nope. Do you want to, my love?"

"I don't know. Do I?" Trick giggled, wondering how much better she could possibly feel than she already did.

A clear shot was brought to her that she took without much regard. A yelp came from the kitchen. "Not that one! That was mine!" Bill called Joel back to the kitchen and he returned with a glass of water tall enough to choke a horse.

"Bill says drink this whole thing. Right away," Joel looked very serious.

"Why? What'd I do?" she said blearily.

"Nothing. Oh, you're so cute!" he pinched her cheeks. "I accidentally gave you his shot."

"Shit," she looked around the floor like she had dropped an earring.

"You'll be fine. But he says you have to drink this whole thing. For your stomach."

"Oh," she beamed at him and he kissed her, hard. She drank the glass of water like a good patient, sitting back to wait for the affects of something she had heard was a gay drug, a date rape drug, to kick in. She knew she was safe in Joel's care, relatively, yet still she braced herself. The love he had for her was something she was counting on right now, if only for now. The guy didn't pay his taxes. "How can I marry you? You
222

aren't a responsible citizen!" she'd berate him and she was quite serious about it, which always pissed him off. There was more to life than taxes, according to Joel.

Gigi sauntered over, laughing at Trick's condition. "You having any fun yet?"

"Yes!" she replied. "You?"

"I'm home!" She grabbed Trick's hands and peeled her off the chaise lounge chair, dancing with her, rubbing the sheer fabric of her shirt that was damp from sweat against Trick's chest. Gigi gave her bedroom eyes and Trick responded in kind, the two turning each other on as the drugs fulfilled its duty. Trick sat down suddenly, feeling too dizzy to stand. She couldn't feel her legs. Joel saw this and approached.

"How you feeling, baby?"

"Amaaazing," she slurred. "Wow!" Then she inadvertently slumped over, messy. He tried to encourage her to get back up and dance, but her legs were completely unable to support her. She couldn't even keep her head upright.

"You two! In the bathroom with me. Now!" Bill shouted, as he jumped in place like Richard Simmons on a wild, drug-fueled tirade. Joel helped her up, her body now completely useless. She wondered how it could possibly be that she was walking. She had no sensation in her legs, but the rest of her was feeling so good that everything about this whole loss-of-body function thing was funny to her.

"Where are you taking me?" she said almost inaudibly, giggling.

"Bill wants us. Pronto."

They entered the immaculate marble bathroom and shut the door behind them. Bill busied himself with filling the bathtub. "Take her clothes off. You're hot and she's gorgeous. Let's take a bath."

Joel tried to find the clasp to Trick's skirt. Without his support, she slid down to the floor, her world a total blur. "Joel? Joel, what's happening? I don't want to take a bath," her voice was small and remote.

Joel stopped and looked to Bill who shut off the water and approached them. He sized them up. "You love this girl?" he asked.

"Sure. She's great, man," Joel replied.

"Hey, little girl, you like this guy here?"

"What did he say?" Trick was confused. Their voices seemed very far away. She looked for Joel through her

224

fog. Joel continued to look at Bill, waiting to see where this was going.

"Well, as I see it, you all have had fun at my expense. So let's get going. It would be so hot to watch her suck your cock. Can you manage that?"

Joel took a minute to register what was being said, his own brain fogged by consumption. He reached down and unfastened his pants and maneuvered his penis into Trick's lolling mouth.

"No, no! Not like that! Pick her up! She looks disgusting!"

Bill helped Joel turn her over and propped her up on her hands and knees to face Joel, who got down on his knees, facing her. He fumbled to get his semi flaccid penis into her mouth, the drugs and his Jewish guilt getting the best of him. Bill lifted her flowery skirt and awkwardly pushed his small dick, wet with his own spit, into her ass. She groaned underneath the new pressure she felt. To the men, she seemed to be enjoying herself. So they continued without another word until Bill came in her ass with such force that it knocked Joel out of her unresponsive mouth without recourse. He lifted her up off the floor and dragged her out without a look behind them.

Joel felt suddenly sick and decided it was time to get the hell out of there. Trick was barely conscious. Bill, seeing them head for the door, insisted on walking them out. As they got into the elevator, without anything coherent to say, Bill whipped out his small penis in the middle of the elevator, leaving it out as they descended the floors of the building, an unpleasant surprise waiting for that unsuspecting someone hoping to catch the next elevator. They were quite a sight. Luckily, the elevator car did not stop. When they were outside and saying their garbled goodbyes, Bill pulled down his pants and exposed his ass the entire duration it took them to walk the block to the nearest avenue to retrieve a cab. They looked back every couple of feet to see him bent all the way forward, full moon in view of a neighbor walking her puff ball of a dog at that ungodly hour. It was all too bizarre to find any humor in it.

Things changed dramatically for Teresa after that night. She woke to the real-life nightmare that she had been raped, on Joel's watch for that matter, further confirming she could trust no one. She had known Joel was a scumbag at the end of the day, out only for himself

226

and his good time, but this was a whole new level of betrayal. She absolutely refused Joel's phone calls. Whatever they had been, it was over. The hardest part, though, was admitting to herself that she had allowed this to happen by placing herself in a defenseless situation. That was what disgusted her the most.

Brad, the personal trainer, had decided to stay over that night, Bill turning him onto the pipe, and that started Brad's stint with crystal meth that would last a long, hard month, transforming his body into a skeleton, destroying his nerve endings and hollowing his soul. When Teresa ran into him again, a month later, she didn't recognize him. She couldn't believe he was the same man. He was on a dance floor at some club moving to the music like a skinny idiot, a completely different person. His face was gaunt, his brain Swiss cheese. He didn't even remember meeting her before. How could she save him? She was sadly realizing there was no saving any of them.

And as Teresa began her process of rescinding affection for the now hopeless, she paused to reflect yet again: what is so important about these people and why should I care if they sink or swim? Who am I to judge? This world had never stopped ceasing to produce utter chaos around her own life that feasted on her tired body. She knew she was worth more, that this world could be beautiful. But her spirit had been sufficiently drained. No part of her seemed to care anymore.

Sitting in her apartment, alone, Teresa felt empty. "What else is there?" she wondered out loud. It started to become an old question. Must I continue to feel this way? What damage am I really doing to myself and how can I stop it? Am I blowing it? It seemed so long ago that she felt happy and the questions sounded absurd, to a lone figure talking to itself. The truth was, she didn't know what happiness was anymore. The self-judgment exhausted her, but she knew it was coming from her instincts for a reason. Stop dousing your field of vision, she'd tell herself. Stop polluting yourself. But the likelihood of having a future filled with genuine happiness and a family of her very own seemed too far to grasp. She suspected that who she would eventually become was more to see than meets the eye, yet she was fresh out of ideas and needed
228

cash to survive adequately. "It's time to get back to work," she said with a rasp that had deepened with the day and the pit in her soul.

Chapter 8

James lets himself in with his set of keys and walks quickly towards Emma who is asleep in bed. He carries a dress on a hanger covered in plastic. He reaches over her and roughly shakes her awake. "Hey, Em, you have to get up and get ready. I had Suzy get your black dress dry-cleaned. The car will be here in an hour." He stops shaking her and moves away from the bed. Emma wakes, unable to focus her eyes. She gets up and shuffles to the bathroom, shutting the door without a word.

James and Emma sit in the back seat of a black Town Car. Emma is staring listlessly out the side window. James is shouting into his cell phone. "Tell him I'm out of the office until tomorrow! And if that's not good enough for him, 'fuck you' always works!" James hangs up the phone. "I need to take the nipple outta that guy's mouth," he spat. "These shallow writers with trust fund pacifiers never learned the lesson that other people work for a living."

Emma scoffs and leans closer to the window as she pulls out a flask from her purse and takes a swig.

"You doing alright, Em?" he turns, taking a harder look at her.

"No," Emma looks through the front window, then back through the side window, growing frantic. There is broken glass littering the side of the road. "Why the fuck did we come this way, James? This is where it happened!"

"Well shit, Emma. I think this is the day to deal with it. I mean, why spread the pain out? This is good for you."

"Don't tell me how to mourn, you insensitive prick!" Emma sits back in her seat, exasperated. She pauses, looking blankly forward. She takes another pull from the flask. "Why did I wear this dress?" Emma is on the verge of tears.

James remarks snidely, "That whiskey's not going to change your outfit."

She glares at him then chooses to ignore him. Her attention follows a memory train. "You know, Dad used to be hard on us kids. When Christopher was little, it was beautifully exemplified on camera, for all to see. My Dad loved that stupid camcorder. And during one of those glorious home videos, he decided to berate him. He was just a little boy," she stops to take a moment, the image coming into focus. "It was during a heat wave. The house had no air-conditioning and we were all fed up with each other. The humidity made it unbearable. Dad started yelling for no reason and unleashed on Christopher. I remember he couldn't say the word bus. He was only two and he would say 'bu bu bu' over and over. He was so adorable. But Dad got so frustrated that he tore the toy bus away, and Christopher's face fell, the look of pure sadness. But," she pauses briefly and snaps her index finger in the air to accentuate, "he didn't cry. He just dropped his head onto the couch face first, arms at his sides. He couldn't

232

understand what was happening, but his world had crumbled anyway," Emma is having trouble composing herself. "I never wanted to see him as sad as I saw him that day, his two year old self. Never," she looks down at nothing.

The sun is shining brightly. The Town Car pulls up in front of the steps leading to a small, Gothic-style, Pentecostal stone church. On the steps are four large men with walkie-talkies directing people into the church as if it were a nightclub. There is a crowd of people formed in front of the church's front doors and Emma is taken aback that she doesn't recognize the people in attendance. They stare at Emma as she and James push their way through.

Once inside the doors, Emma turns to James, grabbing at his collar. "Who are these fucking people? I don't see anyone I know!" her voice grows frantic.

"Emma, stay calm," James grabs her arm to guide her further in.

The interior is a vast auditorium, with a banner reading "God Is Love" displayed across the stage, front and center. There is a hushed tone as people are ushered into their seats. The church houses three hundred people at maximum capacity and it is filling up quickly.

Emma sees Ron, who has scratches covering his face and wears a gigantic leg cast. She rushes to him and gives a big hug. Ron can barely speak. "I'm... I'm so sorry, Emma."

"Shhh. Don't, Ron. It won't bring him back. What's done is done. Please don't say anymore. I know you loved him," Emma releases Ron's grasp before she loses her composure and says or does something she'll regret. She marches towards the front row with James hurrying after her. They sit on the opposite side of her mother, a petite, blonde woman with a look that is surprisingly calm, sitting with immediate family. Emma takes a deep breath and looks around for her father. The place is a sea of strangers. She turns back to front and whispers in James's ear, "So stoic, my mother. Like she didn't abandon us emotionally after Dad left. I love how death brings us all closer together, you know? All one big happy family."

"Is your Dad here?"

"I would fucking hope so. It would be just like him to lurk in the back and leave early."

Those in attendance finally take their seats. Emma shifts uncomfortably, as technical difficulties with the organ music put her on edge. She takes another pull from the flask. James puts his hand on her lap to reassure her. She ignores it. She sits, motionless, staring at the pulpit.

The pastor, a man in his forties, takes the stage. He is a heavyset man with a beet red complexion. He wears a sensible suit and a sunny demeanor. He begins with, "Thank you all for coming. I want to welcome you all, Christopher's family and friends. And look, even George is here, Christopher's father."

234

Emma's head whips around, looking to where the pastor has indicated. She spots George Montgomery, a big man in an unassuming suit, employing a defeated air. He sits ten rows back, off to the side with a blonde woman, a younger version of her mother. His pained expression forsakes a certain embarrassment for being singled out. The woman sitting next to him is surprised by the acknowledgment, visibly delighted, then gloats.

The pastor continues, "I never met Christopher. But I know from meeting his mother and his relatives that Christopher was a loving and deeply spiritual and religious person. And he welcomed the Lord Jesus Christ into his life."

Emma is unable to fully register what he is saying.

"Let's not try to understand how he died, but how he lived. And appreciate the time we've spent. Let's enjoy the time he gave us all. That God will receive him with open arms into his Kingdom. That he will be merciful. May all the souls of those departed rest in peace. Amen." There are a few 'Amens' from the audience. The pastor goes on. "It's a sad day when someone is ripped from our lives, as Jesus was ripped from the lives of his followers and five hundred of his closest friends. They could have gone home that day. They could have been with their families. Instead, they chose to stand by the word of Jesus. Because they weren't liars. They weren't deceivers. Sure, you may say Jesus was a charlatan. He was a con man. A liar. But they knew Jesus to be true. They saw the wounds. The nails sticking out. The blood dripping from his hands. Ask them. They're all still here. Alive. Christopher will be welcome, because he has accepted the Lord Jesus. Those who have not..."

Emma stands up. "What the fuck is this?" she shouts.

The pastor stops and looks in the direction of her voice. Emma whips her head towards her mother then turns back towards the pastor. "Who hired you? Did they pay you for this? Christopher wasn't a born again. He didn't believe in this God shit. He was a good boy, on his way to becoming his own man," she says, her voice cracking. She leaves her seat and starts moving towards the pastor.

James stands and follows, trying to coax Emma from nearing the pulpit. "Uh, Em..." he chirps.

"He was full of life. He wasn't worried about dying and meeting Jesus. Like all of you," she pauses along the way, swinging her hands around to make a grand gesture, then stops to address her mother. "Because you don't know what you're living for. You can't step outside of yourself to see any of us for who we really are. You're too busy judging others. Because you're a coward. All of you!"

Her mother gasps and holds her hand over her mouth. Emma's register drops as she continues. "Mother, you were wrong to do this. Christopher deserved better. When we were young, what were so you worried about losing if you weren't worried about losing us?" Her mother stammers. Emma turns to the pastor. "It wasn't like you knew him. Obviously there's money to be

236

made here. Isn't it time to pass around the basket? In the name of Jesus? Or Saint Christopher?"

James approaches her, interrupting softly, "Emma? Let's go. Jesus has left the building. Next round's on me."

She gives one last desperate look to her father, who sits quietly staring ahead. She shakes her head, disarmed. A security guard comes forward and grabs her shoulders, trying to forcibly usher her out. She wrangles out of his grasp, dropping her purse in the scuffle, gives him the middle finger right to his face, and walks out. James picks up her purse and follows her out, head down. There is a stir from the audience as the crowd is left unsettled.

Tony's is one of the original neighborhood bars in the heart of Little Italy. There are a few tables and wooden chairs scattered around the saw-dusted floor. "That's Life" by Frank Sinatra plays on the jukebox. Tony, the bartender and proprietor, chews on a cigar. A man in his seventies, Tony has seen it all.

Emma walks in and takes a spot at the bar next to a morbidly obese man engaging in conversation with the man himself. She interrupts them to order a drink, "Hey, Tony. Maker's Mark up. Double. Don't let me see the bottom of the glass."

Tony gives her a wave of the hand as he slowly makes his way to the till. "Sure thing, dollface," he grits his teeth to keep the cigar in place. The drink is poured and placed in front of her. She grabs the glass and almost empties it in one long draw.

The obese man responds in turn. "Yeah! Me too, Tony! Never let me see the bottom of my glass ever again."

Tony reaches for the house vodka bottle. He refills the pint glass in front of the guy, no ice or mixer, all the way to the top. The obese man chuckles and peers to his side at Emma. "Hey! You look different today. Somebody die?"

She looks at him with disdain. She struggles to speak, but cannot.

"I'm right! I've seen that distant look in the eye before," he laughs and takes a big gulp of his drink.

Tony steps in. "Don't listen to this guy," he offers.

A patron from the back of the bar calls out, "Hey, Tony. They ever gonna open that place across the street?"

"Eh, who knows? I see a lotta equipment going in there," Tony offers and walks to the front window, chewing on his cigar.

The obese man continues to stare at Emma. He points to her drink, "I used to drink whiskey. By ten, the wheels would come off. I couldn't steer my way home, you know? And who wants to be home by ten?"

"Certainly not a drunk, " Emma's reply is snotty.

"I was born inta hell. You shoulda met my motha before she was beaten to death. What a woman."

"I bet."

"Great lookin'. But sure couldn't pick 'em."

"A lot of women seem to have that problem," Emma cocks her head in his direction.

"My fatha used to kill people. He didn't care. I was, like, a little kid. You don't really figure it out til you're older what all that mopping up a tha floor was and the popping a tha caps. And your motha cryin'. But I'll never forget that far away look in the eye."

"My brother was just killed in a car accident."

"Oh, I'm so sorry, sweetheart. That's terrible. I never had a brother."

"How come there are no swimming pools in Cuba?"

"Huh?"

"Because those that can swim live in Miami," Emma says dryly.

The obese man bursts out laughing, almost busting his guts. She offers a half-smile and drinks heartily. He drinks too, downing the whole pint. Seeing this, she recoils. "Remind me no more jokes. Wouldn't want the wheels to fall off," she slurs her words more than she expected or wanted to.

He slams the glass down. "I'm drivin' you home today, baby. I finally got you to talk to me. Next stop, Pleasantville."

"Oh, dear."

"The name's Rockets Redglare."

"That's some name. Nice to meet you, Rockets Redglare," she throws out a hand. He takes it and they shake.

"I've gotten a lot of joy fightin' with my vices. I came to realize I'll never be normal. I'd love to buy ya a drink, you know, when my luck turns around."

"How about I buy you a drink?"

"You free on Thursday nights? I do stand-up comedy. I buy different books, and I hide my jokes in the cover. After the act, I give the book away. Without the jokes inside, of course. I'm looking for donations right now."

"I have some books I'll never read again," she turns to Tony, "Hey Tony? Can we get a refill?" She downs the rest of her glass and pushes it forward. "You know what I have always hated? Men who don't know the difference between conversation and sex. I have never understood why men are so unable to engage a woman in conversation without masking everything they have to say, about anything, without sex as the goal."

"Your problem is... What's your name again?"

240

"I never gave it. It's Emma."

"Emma, there's time in a guy's life, you know, where he gets the chance to talk to a beautiful girl, like you, and he risks all self-esteem. All for that chance to steal another encounter with you. Guys are, like, dumb enough to think that the talking means that the girl is interested in him."

"Guys want women to be interested in them. To talk," she laughs.

"No. Guys know that all women are whores. They just want the best looking whore."

Tony refills their glasses and Rockets Reglare palms the pint glass in his fat mitt, drinking half of it. "You know, the doctor told me I got three months left to live if I keep drinking like this. My mother told me when I was, like, six, or three, that the doctors told her I wasn't going to live past..." he stops himself, shaking his head. "You're dealt that hand and what do you do, sit there waitin' to lose? Nah, you bet against the house. Me? I'm always lookin' to double down. I'm due for a win."

"What will that win get you? More rounds? A better looking whore? Good for you. I have this garbage truck outside my window. It's fucking loud. Pisses me off. Because I have to listen to it. Fuck this city. And fuck you," Emma gets up to take a piss. Rockets Redglare stares straight ahead.

Emma emerges from the dingy bathroom. She catches herself swaying and straightens herself to make it back to the bar, where Rockets Redglare still sits, white-knuckling his pint glass. She rummages through her purse for cash, frustrated.

"Hey, it's okay. We've all been mistaken for trash," Rockets Redglare smiles innocently. "It's not necessarily how much noise it makes. It's whether people notice or not that it's gone in the morning."

Emma squeezes her eyes tightly. My brother's gone, she says to herself. He's really gone. She fishes out a hundred dollar bill and slams it down on the bar. "Goodbye," she manages and staggers out.

Emma exits a local deli, clutching a forty-ounce beer in a brown paper bag. She walks slanted down the empty streets of lower Manhattan, heading further down.

The large boardwalk of the Brooklyn Bridge is empty, its steel wire suspension arching upwards, quietly framing the East River. The whir of the speeding cars on the roadway below creates a noise that blankets the morning. She creeps towards the center of the bridge and sits on the iron handrail. She takes a long drink from the bottle of beer and looks across the length of the east river towards the end of Manhattan, then down to the water below.

The sun starts to rise, filling the sky with stark, white light and illuminating the steel borders of the structured

242

edifices that make up the island of Manhattan beyond. She is beholden by its magnificence. Cars hum beneath her, deafening everything around her. Emma sits still and stolid.

8. Out of Dodge

Teresa got the news from her aunt. Her mother was gone, liver failure. It happened suddenly, and Teresa had been too high to pay attention to the signs. Her mother had called several times but she never answered and her mother never left any messages telling her what was really going on. She didn't want to upset her daughter with such awful news, knowing her Teresa was making it in that big city and she didn't want to be a nuisance. Teresa thought that if her sweet, beloved mother knew the truth, it would've killed her sooner. There were no words to assign meaning, just an empty cavity deep in her chest that needed filling. She couldn't reach down deep enough to address the clawing inside her ribcage. She felt a burning in the cavities of her eyes, but they were unable or unwilling to form tears. Instead, her eyes felt dry and hollow in their sockets because she had become a shell of her former self. No one could help her navigate through this paramount loss, so profound, because her actions of late caused a certain resignation to feel abysmal about everything. So many bad choices, such removal from home and heart and hearth. "I deserve this," she thought.

Donnie had gotten wind of her mother passing and offered to help. "Darling, you must get well. You've gone through a serious tragedy. Take some time away," he said earnestly into the phone. She was half-listening, but agreed nonetheless to his offer of financing a trip out of the city, to any destination she chose. After hanging up the phone, a tiny pang of promise stirred in her, a feeling she hadn't had in a long while. The thought of breaking free from the confines of this concrete jungle created an excitement in her and she knew she needn't second-guess it. She was remiss. Things had gotten so far out of hand that she had stopped trusting her own instincts. She lost anchor and was out to sea, for real this time. She heard from a friend that Thailand had a Full Moon party not to be missed. She decided to go for it.

The long flight brought her further away from everything she knew, and she was grateful for that because she just couldn't deal. She was hoping to disappear for a while. She had no set plans, shy of meeting up with some friends along the way, and figured she'd work it out when she got there.

Bangkok is a crazy city, full of noise and traffic that puts New York to shame. She chose a hotel near the airport to recover from the jetlag, setting out the next day to inspect the red light district of Patpong out of sheer curiosity. She felt fearless at every turn and because her life hadn't made sense for so long, she figured she might as well dive in and experience something new. In her estimation, she had already been through the worst of it. It was time to kick start her well-worn instincts in a new land. Nothing was going to harm her now because she decided to have her own back.

She walked through the seedy edge of the night market, uninterested in acquiring any souvenirs. She had decided in advance to travel light. The men working the doors of the many sex clubs would come out onto the street, battling each other for her business. They were annoyingly aggressive, rushing out onto the street to meet her. She wasn't particularly impressed with each hard sell, so she waited for the one that appeared the most sanguine. That guy always had what to offer. He simply nodded his head in her direction and, pleased with his assurance of a good time found within, she made her way towards the entrance.

Inside was nothing she had ever seen before. Every working girl was completely nude, and because it was still early, they surrounded her, their rail-thin figures pressed up against her from every direction, offering her a "Drink? Drink?" She was instantly overwhelmed but played it cool. She chose a table near the stage and ordered a whiskey. There were few others, all men, at the many tables spread out over the big room, covered in Thai girls who were waiting on them hand and foot. It was as unsettling as it was fascinating.

The show began soon after. First up was one of the young, beautiful Thai girls, still naked of course, as if putting clothes back on was remotely an option. She grabbed from a bowl of water filled with ping-pong balls, got on all fours facing up and out like a crab, and
246

placed one of the little white balls in her vagina and popped it out. It flew across the room. Trick was amazed at its distance! She looked down at the young woman's feet and saw a ping-pong paddle, inviting participation. Trick downed the whiskey she was given and threw enough baht, the monetary unit in Thailand, on the table to more than cover the cost. She approached the stage and grabbed the paddle. As the young woman popped a ball from her woman's part, Trick returned the serve, sending the ball in the direction of the men, at any given table. With each pluck, she struck a few of them hard and laughed herself silly at their reactions. The balls were wet from the water in the bucket, yet the men were hollering in disgust as if they were being splashed with secretion. Trick congratulated herself on her near-perfect aim.

The next girl wrote her name with a pen on a piece of construction paper. And the next, blew out candles on a birthday cake. The next took the same crab-like stance, this time shoulders arched down to touch the floor, and shot darts out of her vagina to pop balloons that were hung high from the ceiling. Trick thought that she saw it all after that

247

one, thinking the balloons must have been rigged, until the last girl got up.

Coca-Cola bottles in Thailand are much larger than they are in the states, marked red and white. Seltzer bottles are marked only with white. This little girl got on top of a huge, glass bottle of seltzer and tilted her pelvis, emptying the entire contents of the bottle into her body. Trick thought, where the hell is she putting that? Then, she stood above an empty cola bottle, with the red and white markings, and began filling it with cola, brown fluid, bubbles and all. She did it twice. Trick stood there, inches from the stage, flabbergasted. This was beyond her scope of reasoning. It was time to go.

The next day was the Thai New Year. Once outside your hotel, you were subjected to the kind of dousing with water that put every water fight you've ever had as a child to bed. You couldn't even walk ten feet without getting repeatedly drenched. She loved it! She sought out an outdoor market that sold water guns and stock piled. She was not letting this opportunity to play pass her by.

As she prepared to fly to Koh Samui to meet with some people Gigi had told her about who were happy to put her up for the next few days, with designs on taking a boat to the Full Moon party on Koh Phangan, she readied her guns full of water and entered the airport, shooting everyone in her path. It was pure delight! She had a pack on her back full of water, and single shot water pistols on either side, the massive water gun connected to the pack with pump action never leaving her hands. Her travel bag was light and easy to carry and then drop when she saw someone worth dousing. It was the most fun she had ever had at an airport.

Once on Koh Samui, she met up with the others staying at the house on the water of an expat who had left behind a family, never to be heard from again. There were many of those in Thailand. She was not here to judge, only to play. Their host was instantly challenged by her and grabbed violently at her gun, causing the skin to rip off her palm as she fought him off. She was outraged. Why the fuck was he trying to take away her fun? When they got to the house, she excused herself to cool off and take a nap in one of the many rooms. She knew the night would be long and needed to recharge, the fresh bandage on her left hand an indication their host was not friend but foe, making her feel less safe in her surroundings. One of his friends had taken a liking to her, helped wrap her hand, but she wanted nothing to do with any of them. She was not to be had by anyone. Not this trip.

When she woke from her nap, she dressed in her white, silky dress and joined the rest for dinner. She waited on the lanai, breathing deep and taking in the beautiful view of the water, a massive statue of Buddha in the far distance. She contended she was not going to let this expat heathen, nor anyone, ruin her good time. When it was time to sit, she chose the seat at the end of the long, wooden table, across from the host, because no one else had. Her excitement extinguished her appetite. When the food was served, the host looked up from his plate, saw her refusal to eat, and audibly growled in her direction. She laughed. He wiped his mouth with the back of his hand and cleared his throat. Addressing the table, he made a threatening speech about how strict they were about drugs in Thailand and that no one, under any circumstance, should ask anyone for drugs under any circumstance, that if they were caught,

250

the punishment was the death penalty. She got up and walked across the table, placing the wrapped gift she'd been holding in her good hand to the right of his plate. The gesture produced an odd look from him. The wrapping contained a small, sterling silver box with etchings on its exterior and savvy flip lid, something she had purchased back in the states. Inside held a tiny silver spoon. She returned to her seat at the opposite end of the table and watched him tear at the paper. No money had been discussed regarding her stay with these people; she was here merely on Gigi's referral. The least she could do was come bearing a gift. When he realized what it was, his face lit up. He loved it. In fact, immediately after opening it, he pulled out his private stash of cocaine and dumped it directly into the box, using the tiny silver spoon to service himself a bump of the white powder. He leered at her and she took that as a thank you, got up, and walked out the room. Fuck you, she thought. I have an open wound in a foreign country because of you. I hope you choke on your coke, you animal.

When everyone finally rallied to leave, they had to find a boat that would take them to Koh Phangan, as it was late and the last ferry had since departed. They paid some locals to take them over in a speedboat, and Trick positioned herself at the bow. The fresh, cool wind whished by her face and whipped at her dress and she devoured it. Nothing impeded her view and the speed with which they traveled exhilarated her. She was afraid of nothing.

The island was exploding with energy. Not only was it the Full Moon party, but it was also the Thai New Year, and the combination brought tens of thousands of people from all over the world. The music was electric, as was the vibration of everyone in attendance. Someone from her group ordered a drink that came in a red plastic bucket, the kind children play with at the beach, very fitting of their location. Because of its large size, they decided to share. After they all took a few swigs of its contents, they began playfully dancing on the sand. A display of fireworks exploded above their heads, as a Happy New Year's sign lit up, lighting the night sky. Then, they experienced a collective kind of blackout. When she came to, the sun was coming up, and her new friends were in pieces. One of the girls had her purse stolen and the general consensus
252

was that they had been drugged because no one could remember the last few hours. Trick didn't care. She felt great! Her passport and cash had never left her tightly wound clutch, attached to her good hand at all times. They wanted to leave. She was not ready for that. In her mind, the party was just getting started, as the music continued to sail across the beach, the partygoers in full swing. Her group grew annoyed with her and took off, leaving her to venture out on her own. Good riddance, she thought.

The first thing she did was eyeball the crowd. She picked out the biggest looking badass of the group, a dark skinned woman wearing a hefty cowboy hat. She walked right up to her. "Are you a cop?" she said.

The woman turned and said, "Yeah," with a laugh.

"Do you know where I can get some E?"

The woman laughed so loudly that people stopped dancing and turned. When she stopped laughing, she turned on Trick. "Come with me," she said sternly.

Trick followed her into town thinking, I must be mad. What the hell am I doing? This is insane! The woman led her into a bar, walked right up to the counter and said a few Thai words to the bartender, who disappeared into the back. When he returned, she asked Trick for an amount of baht that she quickly relinquished to the woman, who then handed the bills to the bartender, who then passed over two pills. The woman kept one for herself and handed one to Trick and they toasted the pills by clanking them together, washing them down with a shot of whiskey. It was too surreal for words.

They returned to the party, jumping into the water and playing with sea cucumbers, the white, sticky substance the creatures produced when rubbed covered Trick and she laughed her head off. The bright morning light reflected off the water and she paused, thinking of how much her Mama would have loved this. She smiled into the sun, remembering her mother as a young woman, fearless and beautiful. And that thought brought her so much sober joy.

After, she joined the cowgirl cop and her friends for an after party that took place in a massive tree house. If she thought the music was good at the Full Moon party, the music in the tree house tripled it in its excellence. She danced with the coolest kids in the world. She was moved by every one of them, glory be
254

theirs. It was the most delicious feeling she had ever felt.

When the party was coming to a close, she forged her way through the grassy dunes, away from the goodness of the tree house and beyond. She had no idea where she was exactly, but knew she had a ferry to catch. She walked the beach under the bright sun for a time, not even sure she was traveling in the right direction, until she found the ferry dock. Glory be. With time to spare, she ventured into town to have her wound redressed at a Thai clinic. They were kind to her and gave her healing salve and charged her close to nothing for their service. She loved them for caring for her. What a blessed land.

The ferry ride back was like an assembly of the United Nations. No one spoke because no one needed to. Every face looked out at another with smiles of real bliss. She sat on the line of benches built into the sides of the boat, looking at each beautiful face and knew that they had all won. There were those who made it to the Full Moon party on the beach and those who had made it to the tree house after party. Every pair of eyes she locked onto knew they had won an unspoken prize of connectedness and triumph. They had made it here, a profoundly beautiful place this world has to offer, and made the most of it. It was wonderful to be of this world. The peace found in the smiles was unforgettable.

When the ferry docked, her reverie subsided. She immediately panicked. She had no idea where the house was located, had no address. Not that she was in any hurry to confront the expat heathen, nor the crew that abandoned her. But she had to get the rest of her shit. What an oversight, she thought, and a laugh actually escaped her. The Thai cab drivers on motorbikes hollered aggressively at those disembarking. She had no idea where she was going, but got on the back of one of the bikes anyway. She used her hands to indicate a direction, not even sure if it was the right one. Regardless, it was a good day for a ride.

As the motorbike made it's way on the windy road, she looked out at the water, smiling. She was alive with the wind through her hair and she was happy. She finally felt free of all entanglements, found in the exploration of the unknown. Then, miraculously, she saw in the distance, the large Buddha statue across the water and she calculated its angle until she discerned the house's location from the view she remembered looking out from the terrace. She found the house! Suspending her panic had made it a real breeze to find, after all. She paid the man more than his asking price in baht and walked into a house that was up in arms. The guy who had shown interest in her had worried she had been killed or hurt, so much so he had called the police to find her, garnering concern from the rest. She found it all so completely ridiculous and deemed them all sour grapes for leaving early in the first place. She grabbed her shit and got the hell out of there. Amateurs, she thought, with a toss of her hair.

Chapter 9

Emma walks in with bags full of groceries. She looks rested and appears calm. She checks her messages as she puts the food away in their respective cabinets. A familiar voice fills the room.

"Hi, it's Gigi. It's been so long! Sorry I haven't called sooner. But I'm calling you now! Things have been just crazy! You and I have a lot to talk about, girl. I'm sick of missing you. I want to see you! Eddie and I really want you to have dinner with us one night soon. Okay? Call me back!" Her message ends with a beep.

Emma stares at the phone and smiles wistfully.

A car picks up Emma from her front door. Gigi and her husband, Eddie, step out to embrace her warmly. The car takes them to Gigino's, an Italian restaurant all the way at the tip of Manhattan, with an unimpeded view of the Statue of Liberty. They exit the car and walk towards the restaurant, Gigi grabbing Emma's arm to steer her towards Luke, a handsome, well-dressed man who is waiting for them outside the restaurant. He is a college buddy of Eddie's.

Emma gives Gigi a dirty look, "You didn't tell me I'd be entertaining tonight." Emma is not amused.

Gigi squeals, "You know I can't help myself! I didn't think you'd mind. Since when did you swear off meat?"

The guys overhear and look at each other, smirking. "Eddie knows I'm always willing to take one for the team," Luke says with an award-winning smile.

"Fuck this. I'm not ready for this. Could you have found a bigger asshole?" Emma gives Eddie a disappointed look and turns to go, searching for an available cab.

Eddie physically stops her with his body. He speaks under his breath, "Come on, Emma. Sure, he's an idiot. But he's a big deal. Family money. And he's good to look at, the perfect punching bag. And," he winks at her, "he's leaving town soon, so he won't be around long enough for the bruises to surface."

"You remember how much I love a good fight. That means a lot to me," Emma meets his eyes, smiling through her snicker.

Luke approaches cavalierly, "You wouldn't dare deprive me of staring at your nipples all night."

Emma rolls her eyes. "Oh, good. You're going to make this easy," she chides and reluctantly follows them inside.

The table is arranged so that Emma and Luke are sitting across from each other. The waiter is at the table and Luke is ordering, "Can we get an order of the Caprese salad to start? And a large bottle of sparkling water. Does everyone want wine? I've had such a great day. Let's start with cocktails. Emma, you especially look like you could use a drink."

260

"What was so great about your day, Hotshot?" Emma says, looking at her menu.

"Life is good. God is smiling on me. I made a lot of money today."

"So, I guess dinner's on you," she baits him.

Luke looks up, mildly surprised, "But of course!"

"Super. They have a fifty year old single malt scotch here that is one of my favorites."

"Make it two. Let me taste what my money's buying," he says with a carefree grin, making him even more attractive.

Gigi turns to the waiter, "I'll have a Cosmo."

"A Ketel One martini for me. Up, please," Eddie says, finishing the drink order and the waiter leaves. Everyone falls strangely silent. Eddie picks up the ball, "I got the sailboat downtown. Remember when we docked at the Water Club last year and Gigi lost her top? We all can go out on Sunday, if you have time."

"Is this one of those forty-five dollars per head, or is this a corporate event?" Luke callously tears into the bread that's been placed on the table by a busboy.

"Ooh, Mr. Big Spender," Emma's offers the snide remark as an aside.

Gigi breaks the growing tension by hopping up and down in her seat, "I need some sun! Let's go!"

"CNBC rented the boat for two weeks and they're paying for the slip in the harbor for the whole month of June. It would be just us," Eddie says nonchalantly.

Luke turns to Emma, "Will you be joining?"

"That all depends on if I can stand you after tonight."

"You know, your people skills are tremendous," Luke surmises. "I was sitting here wondering why such a beautiful woman as yourself wasn't already spoken for. You made cracking that code easy."

"Keep your fingers out of the cage. I bite," Emma warns.

The waiter arrives with their drinks. Luke holds up his glass, "Here's to my favorite couple in New York City. Through their trials and tribulations, you've shown us it's possible to stick by someone whether they win or lose."

Gigi lets out a squeal and gazes adoringly at Eddie, who leans in to plant a kiss on her pretty lips. They all toast and drink. Gigi sits abruptly in her chair. "Oh my god! I got another tattoo. Wanna see it?" she unbuttons the top of her blouse and exposes her pushed-up-by-a-lacey-bra tits to reveal Eddie's name tattooed across the top of her voluptuous left breast. beautifully executed, albeit hard to read under the dark lights.

"What does it say?" Emma squints to make it out.

"It says Eddie! You can't read it?" Gigi replies, exasperated.

Emma moves in closer to make it out, "Oh yeah. Ok. Wow."

Gigi closes her shirt quickly. She takes a sip from her drink.

Luke interjects, "I think it's very nice. Eddie, you are one lucky man. You always were. Emma, why are you such a buzz kill?"

"Excuse me?"

"Gigi prefaced you as a real party girl. She told me the two of you used to tear it up."

Emma turns to Gigi, "Who the fuck is this guy? What did you tell him?"

"He's someone you'd really like if you would just give him a chance," Gigi snaps. Emma ignores her comment with a wave of her hand. Gigi isn't having any of it, "It's not like you aren't ready to let someone in. As long as I've known you, you've always been so harsh with men. What's up with that?"

"Gigi, enough," Emma gives her a look to freeze blood.

"Fine. I just wish you didn't beat yourself up all the time. You know you deserve to be happy just like everybody else."

"Look, I'm sorry, I'm not very good company. A lot's happened since we last saw each other last. There are some things you don't know about."

Gigi is visibly wounded, "Well, me too! I just started a new position at the magazine. Can you imagine what kind of pressure I'm facing? I read in an article that starting a new job is like one of the most stressful things in life. But I'm out still out enjoying myself, aren't I?"

Emma grows silent.

The food arrives and everyone begins eating quietly.

Luke gets a forkful of food from his plate and offers it to Emma. "Here, taste this," he whispers gently.

She takes it, eyes locked on his. "Oh, wow," she can't help but react to its savory flavor.

"It melts on the tongue, doesn't it?" They stare into each other's eyes. Emma looks away first.

The waiter walks by and Gigi flags him down, "Waiter? Can I have another Cosmo? Anybody?" They shake their heads no. "Well, don't mind if I do!" she says to herself, mostly.

Luke turns to Emma, "Emma, what's going on with your new novel? Gigi told me earlier you're working on something."

"My brother was just killed in a car accident, so I don't know where I stand. In my novel, or in my life."

Gigi drops her fork. "Christopher?" she gasps.

"Yes. Christopher," Emma replies flatly. There is silence. Nobody moves.

Gigi starts to cry. "Oh my God. Oh my God!" she screams, attempting to compose herself by covering her mouth with her hands. Eddie does his best to calm her with a look and a touch.

Luke gently offers, "I'm so sorry, Emma. I lost my mom when I was six. It takes losing the ones closest to us to realize we are not the most important person in our lives."

Emma places her fork down. "Don't," she says, guarded.

"That change will always be there. You can't ignore it. When you get to a place where you can accept it and you're at peace with it, know that that's just the numbness, continuing. Every day you come to terms with a falsified ideal place where there's nothing at stake is dishonest. The feeling that nothing matters because who really gives a shit is the worst place you can be in. It's an excuse for not caring, when in fact, you care very deeply," his smile is soft. "It was only when I knew for certain that I'd lived through something important, something utterly catastrophic, that I was able to come out the other side and realized my life is now worth more because of it. My mother's death gave my life a deeper meaning. Sounds simplistic, I know. But the pain of loss is very real. And we all must find our way out of that pain daily to make the rest of our time here truly matter."

Emma gets up from the table. "Excuse me," she says, as politely as she can muster, and heads for the rest room. Gigi gets up clumsily from the table, banging her knee, and runs after her.

Emma is running cold water on her hands. Gigi enters the bathroom, barely composed. She rushes over to console her, "Oh, I'm so sorry… Oh… Why didn't you tell me? Are you okay?"

"I'm fine."

"He… How… Oh, Em. I don't know what to say. What happened? I mean, how did he…" she is unable to finish her sentence.

"Gigi, he was decapitated on the L.I.E. How can I explain that to you? Can anyone explain that to me?"

"Wow. Oh my God. Who was driving? Not Christopher. He's the best driver ever."

"No, not Christopher.

"Well, then who? Who killed him?"

"No one! It was nobody's fault. It was an accident."

"It has to be somebody's fault! Somebody has to be held responsible!"

"No, Gigi. Life and death just happen," Emma dries off her hands and turns to give Gigi a hug, who seemingly needs it more than she does. "Thank you for introducing me to Luke. I think I'd like to spend more time with him tonight. It's helping me get my mind off things."

"Sure. Of course, babe," Gigi says, drying her eyes.

"I'm going to pick his brain. Nothing too catastrophic."

"I love you, Emma.

"I love you, too. Go back to the table. I'll be there in a minute."

Gigi returns to the table, "Eddie? I wanna go home."

"Are you sure? Okay, baby," Eddie shovels a few more bites of food into his mouth, and throws his napkin on the table.

Gigi addresses Luke, "I'm leaving her in your hands. Don't fuck with her!"

"No worries. I got this," Luke is all confidence.

Emma comes back from the bathroom and sees Gigi and Eddie leaving. "Hey, where are you guys going?"

Gigi gives her a knowing look then wraps her arms around her. "Take care of you," she whispers in her ear.

Emma embraces her back warmly, holding tight.

"It was good seeing you guys. Call me tomorrow. We'll all go sailing," Eddie says.

They all wave good-bye as Emma catches the waiter's attention. "We'll take two more scotches," she adds, "please."

"Very good," the waiter says with a smile and begins clearing the dinner remains.

Emma and Luke stare at each other. Luke breaks the silence, "I was hoping we'd hate each other enough to stay to the bitter end."

"Want to help me finish my novel?"

"When do we start? I'd love to read what you've got so far. Let's get out of here."

"I need to figure out why I should keep writing it. I don't know where it's going. Rookie mistake."

The waiter delivers the drinks and Luke hands him his credit card. He turns to Emma, "What's better? To

268

grow old and shit into a plastic bag, or die when we're supposed to? Young and fearless!"

"I'm all for kicking the shit out of this life," she chimes.

"Better to burn out, then to fade away."

"I knew I liked you. Mostly, I hate people," Emma smirks.

"I'm a likeable guy," Luke gives her his signature smile.

"Uh, oh," she tries her best not to encourage him.

"I'm leaving New York because here people are more interested in their future rather than where they've been."

"Tell me a place that exists where people aren't like that."

"It's all about finding that person who isn't. Then creating a place together, within a place. It can be anywhere in the world."

Emma sighs, "The island to retire on."

"It's about experiencing the known and improving upon it. This city, for me, became all about what's new and different. I became disheartened."

"What's wrong with new? That's what creating is all about."

"I'm taking about love," Luke grabs his drink. "Come on. Let's take a walk. It's a beautiful night." He signs the check the waiter has brought over and grabs her hand. She gives him another look over, grabs her drink and follows his lead.

Emma and Luke walk out into the night, hand in hand. He notices a concrete stairway on the side of the building and leads her by the hand up the stairs to a catwalk overlooking the Hudson River and the Statue of Liberty. They stand together, looking out.

Luke is the first to speak, "Land of the free. Don't we wish we could subscribe to that more often?"

"Another toast?"

"Here's to surviving loved ones lost and finding new ones," he raises his glass and they clink then drink. He sets his glass down on the low railing and moves in closer to her. "Now that I look back on it, the best thing that could've happened to me was my mother dying. It gave me certain liberties to redefine for myself what a woman should be, without living under her shadow."

"How do you figure that?"

He shakes a head that's full of alcohol, cursing his intolerance, and tries to articulate. "Well, without having someone looking over your shoulder all the time, making judgments for you, it's easier to make your own mistakes and learn from them. It gave me that unique chance to carve out my own path. I see you're

270

the same. Come here," he grabs her and pushes her against the railing. He kisses her, hard. She is surprised by it, kisses him back, then stops him with the palm of her hand pressed to his chest.

"I don't think I'm ready for this. But I had a nice time. Thank you."

He leans back, feigning surprise. He eyes her suspiciously. "You're a tough one, Emma. But you may be worth it," he smiles. "Let me walk you to a cab. For another time, perhaps."

The streets seem more empty than usual. She enters her dark, quiet loft, feeling good for having stepped out. The attention Luke showed her was refreshing. Putting down her bag, she heads to the fridge to pour a nightcap and stops at the sound. Breathing. She is not alone in her apartment. "Hello?" she croaks, backtracking to find the light switch with a trembling hand.

"Who is he," the voice says flatly in the dark. His voice betrays how intoxicated he is.

She flips on the light. James is reclining on her couch sloppily. "Jesus, James. You scared the shit outta me!"

"I know you were out with someone. So, who is he? Got yourself a new man to torture, huh Em? Lucky guy," he tries to stand and instead stumbles.

"What the hell are you talking about? You're drunk."

He stabilizes himself and starts slowly walking towards her. "You know," he slurs, "no one is ever going to love you like I do. What a pain in the ass! How does it feel to know you're going to be alone forever?"

"Get the fuck out of my house. Now."

"I've spent so much time here, feels like this place is partly mine," he says with a grand gesture of his hand. "Just tell me, who is he? Did you fuck him yet?"

"What the hell is wrong with you?" Emma tries to push passed him, but James grabs her by the shoulder and they wrestle to the ground. He overpowers her and she uses her legs to kick him off, crawling her way towards to the direction of the front door. He grabs her by one leg, dragging her backwards and flipping her over. He starts punching her head in a flurry of movement, some of the hits landing, but mostly missing. Her legs now freed up, she kicks him again, this time square in the chest, sending him backwards but not down. She scrambles to stand, grabbing an empty whiskey bottle in a bag of trash nearby. She turns and squares off with him. She has never seen this look of anger from him before, as though he was possessed, his screaming mouth a hot, red chasm, his sanity dancing on the edge of bankruptcy. He charges her and, as if in slow motion, she raises the bottle and lands it on the side of his head. He surrenders to gravity, hitting the floor like a full mail sack from the tired shoulder of a letter carrier at Christmastime.

Having no experience in such matters, she feels the need to straighten things up. He'll wake soon, she

272

thought, of course he will. Then, they can make sense of what the fuck just happened here. As she busies herself around the apartment in a shock fog, the sound of pounding shakes her out of her cleaning reverie. She stops moving to be sure she heard, in fact, anything at all. There it is again. Boom boom boom. "This is the police. Open up!" says the voice on the other side of her front door. She looks around wildly, staving off panic. James begins to stir. Well, good, she thinks. At least he's not dead.

She opens the door and does her best to explain that the minor argument she had with her ex boyfriend was just that, minor. The police insist they need to inspect the scene after pointing out that her shirt is soaked with blood. They push the door in. It takes her a more than a moment to realize that she cut her finger on the bottle she broke over the head of another human. She hadn't noticed. Inside, the apartment looks as if someone was indeed murdered. As she had busied herself trying to clean things up, she proceeded to bleed all over everything and hadn't even noticed. This does not look good, she thinks, and offers up her side of things immediately, "He attacked me! I had to defend myself!"

"Ma'am, we understand," referring to the golf-ball sized bump on her forehead she didn't even know was there until after they pointed it out. "We're going to have to take you in anyway for questioning, regardless. You understand how this looks."

"Ma'am? Really?" she scoffs, not pressing the point. "Can I at least change my shirt?" she pleads. She imagines going to jail covered in blood and while that would earn her points in street cred, it looks and feels nasty.

"Yes, but make it quick," the officer responds jointly.

She grabs the first soft thing her hand lands on in her shirt drawer, flannel cut-off shirt, and she is quietly pleased with the choice, as if anything about this situation could be made better. At least I'll look tough, she thinks, as she fumbles with its buttons. Just as the last button is engaged, the cuffs are on her wrists and they escort her out her own front door. She tries to look back to see what has become of her now psychotic agent-turned-ex boyfriend, but is unable to decipher the true mess that has been made.

Being in the back of a cop car is the least fun one can have in one's life. It does not register as real, for one. You can try to make sense of it, but there is no logic to any of it, certainly not if you aren't guilty of anything decidedly tangible. You don't wake up and plan to end your day with the level of chaos "going downtown" provides. It just doesn't add up.

They book her and throw her in a cell with about 10 other women, which was not at all what she imagined jail would be like, not that she ever imagined it. She looks around at the angry, fed up faces, hollering at this and that, all of them loudmouths, spouting off disdain over a lifetime of being victimized by a system that never cared about them. Fat, black crack dealers and skinny, pissed off Puerto Rican chicks with a grudge at the world, at the ready to serve it up. Emma is scared

274

and instantly anxious because the outcome is uncertain here. Fighting any one of them would be messy, and she wasn't in the mood. She takes a seat on an iron bench and waits for hours, listening to their tirades. She breathes evenly, viewing her fellow inmates through slitted eyes, squelching her inherent disdain. I can't judge these women outright, she thinks, but we're all products of our choices and these bitches made some bad ones. Still, they are dangerous as fuck. Best not to piss them off.

As the hours extend, Emma becomes a pressure cooker, not sure how much more of this grandstanding from her fellow inmates she can take. One of the Puerto Rican girls is dangerously close to making good on her threat to kick Emma's ass because she doesn't like her face. Then, by some sort of miracle from the gods, a single, very large cockroach scuttles across the floor, sending the cell's inhabitants screaming and gasping for breath, jumping on top of the iron benches in fear and making quite the scene. Emma stands up suddenly and laughs a deep, belly laugh that releases hours of tension and fear in each heaving chortle. As she laughs, she walks to middle of the room, eyeballing each and every one of these sorry excuses for women. When she is done laughing, she wipes a tear from her eye and exclaims, "Scared of a cockroach. A cockroach! Now, that's rich!" She chuckles all the way back to her seat, kicking at the air in front of her. What a hoot. I dare any one of these bitches to front me now, she thinks. The women avoid her at all costs after that.

She is finally led out of the cell in cuffs and taken outside the building by one of her arresting officers. "Where are you taking me?" she bleats.

"You have to see the DA, before they take you before the judge."

Her heart sinks, as she sees James up ahead, directly in their path. He is dressed in a hospital gown, ass exposed, and has a bandage over his head. He sees her and reacts violently, struggling in cuffs of his own, "What you did is a fucking felony! I could have you put away for a year!"

Her heart sinks into her boots. As she gets closer, she says as calmly as she can muster, "But you won't do that, right? James, I can't be in here for a year. You wouldn't do that."

He struggles and fights the officers trying to detain him as she is quickly redirected into a neighboring building. She shakes her head in disbelief. What the hell happened? As they get closer to the DA's office, the policeman who arrested her stops her for a moment and feeds her some words. 'What?" she gasps.

"This is what he said, so stick with this story. Don't stray from the script. And make sure you apologize. Tell her this will never happen again. This DA is new and has something to prove. She's talking about charging you for felony assault, even if he doesn't press charges. If you can shed some tears, do," he looks up when he sees someone coming down the hallway, and they continue walking. "You know, you opened up his

276

skull. They had to staple it shut," he says under his breath, holding back a smile.

Once inside, Emma softens. She becomes the victim and she is very, very sorry. She assures the DA nothing like this will ever happen again. The DA is young and tight, her pressed suit and sculpted hairdo mean business and Emma can't help but respect her. Still, the thought of where she could end up and how it would most certainly ruin her dictates her every move. She cries her eyes out, hoping to earn much needed mercy. What dignity she had been holding onto at that point flew right out the window.

They lead her into the courtroom, where she is forced to wait for what feels like countless hours. She can see James across the myriad of benches. He looks at her angrily, but much less so. His buzz has most certainly worn off, the reality setting him for him, too. One glance in particular holds a "Let's get the fuck out of here" message from across the room. She knows now he won't let her go down, but that over-achiever DA she isn't so sure about. Although slim, there was still a chance things could go south. Emma's breath remained held.

When it finally comes time for the judge to hear her case, he is made aware that James will not be filing charges against her. The DA comes forward and says she will not be prosecuting, and Emma is released. Her sweet relief is beyond measure. She hightails it out of there and decides its time to wrap things up.

9. Get Out

Trick made fast friends with the Director whose film recently made the rounds in the independent film festival circuit, filling him with newly found pomp and circumstance. He was a real player and she wasn't a gorgeous model, so she wasn't worried about pending advances because his dance card was most certainly full of said models. He was a creative intellectual who was thoroughly enjoying his life, so they got along just fine. She was, after all, fascinated by the human condition, as were most filmmakers, and they never seemed to run out of things to talk about.

He invited her to join a surfing trip to Panama with five of his hardcore surfing buddies. She thought, why the hell not? He's offering to pay for it without the expectation of sex and after her trip to Asia, the adventure of it all called to her senses. She'd never surfed before and thought it a wonderful idea to learn from a pro in a dreamy location. His crew followed the surf, so the waves would be the kind worth tackling. And there was nothing for her in New York at the moment, having departed from her group of "friends" suddenly and indefinitely after her mother passed and her apartment grew smaller by the day. She admitted she just wasn't ready to deal with all that grief. As of now, there was nothing holding her back.

They met at the airport in Panama City, taking different flights from various starting points, but planned well enough in advance that the wait time between arrivals was minimal. They rented a car and waited to load up the boards in the morning, staying at a local hotel for the night to decompress from travel. There was one other girl among the all-male group, Allison, who was a lesbian and Trick liked her instantly. They played cards and drank cheap beer until late into the night in that dingy Panamanian hotel, too excited to sleep with the impending adventure looming ahead.

The Director had a lead foot. After passing through the initial and frightening military checkpoint, they hit the open roads, garnering ticket after ticket, the resolution clearly found in the form of bribes. Trick's Spanish was decent, the only one in the group, from years of paying attention in class, so she worked her magic to talk down the Tombo. The Director was happy to pay for speed racing through the jungle on smooth, windy roads. The day was crisp and clear and beautiful.

They made a home in a village in Bahia that welcomed them warmly. They ate and drank plenty, blanketed by the thick, hot air. The next morning held her first challenge: to get on that board. Rash guard and booties intact, as the massive waves crashed on coral, the Director talked her through it then paddled out by her side. And then she stood up and caught a wave. It was miraculous. She looked over at him with a "Holy shit!" expression and quickly fell off, never to get back up again. No matter. She had felt that exhilaration and she simply could not wait for tomorrow.

The next day they set out on canoes to another island. She had to carry her own board just like everyone else as they walked for over an hour through the jungle in mud so deep her flip-flops became a distant memory. When the trees finally cleared their field of view, the sea and white sand opened before them in picture perfect harmony. No need for booties. This was an uninhabited, white sand oasis with no nasty coral in sight.

She stretched across her chest her wetsuit top and raced out to meet the surf.

Paddling out, she thought that this might be the most perfect day ever. The sky was infinite blue. The water was all theirs. When she got to a place where she thought she could read a wave, she sat up on the board and looked back. Her travel companions and now surfing buddies were all still on the beach, quite a distance away. They stood in a line, looking out at her. She looked behind her for a wave, saw none coming, and decided to paddle back to see what was up. I mean, these guys travel to surf, she thought. Something is definitely up. The idea of a shark crossed her mind, but she refused fear and began swiftly paddling back.

After about an hour, she was incredulous that she remained in the same spot. She would stop paddling occasionally to check in with her compadres who still stood in the same geographical line as before, waving at her, trying to communicate something to her that was getting lost in the tide and the distance that might as well have been miles away. She grew exhausted and confused. What was happening? Why couldn't she swim back? She laid flat on her board and looked up at the crystal blue sky, overcome with a sense of peace. Something was wrong. But, she figured, today was an okay day to die. Mom, I'm sorry I neglected you. Please forgive me. I never meant to let you down.

Suddenly, out of the corner of her eye, she saw the Director swimming towards her without his board. He was splashing around and gasping, struggling much more than he should have. "Swim that way!" he yelled, indicating that she should swim to the far left, away from the beach. She did just that. And slowly, her board washed in. She got to land and hugged the sand. She had gotten caught in a rip tide.

The rest of the trip grew easier. Their accommodations on Bahia were pleasant. The group had their regular breakfast and meeting places. Eventually, and without much budging, the Director seduced her into bed. She enjoyed his attention, but certainly didn't belong to him, even if he was footing the bill. Sex hadn't been a part of that deal, he didn't even know her that way, and she made it very clear that she was there to enjoy herself. She knew once they got back to the states, she
282

would be off his radar. So she acquiesced for the sake of a good time. She certainly didn't expect any love to come from it. And he wasn't bad in bed, but insisted she stare him in the eyes when they came, which registered as a bit creepy to her. She made sure to keep her heart the hell out of it.

There was talk around town of the Party of the Year on a neighboring island and the group was gearing up to go, until a tropical rainstorm hit hard and the Director caught an amoeba from a fruit shake he carelessly ordered, rendering him gravely ill. Trick suspected he was being overly dramatic about it but found it in her heart to deliver him food and drink to his room, to be nice. After all, he had saved her life. He asked her to stay with him, to which she politely declined.

She decided instead to travel into town with Allison to see what the other kids they'd met where up to. They were having a great time palling around together and their current travel companions had all turned to sour grapes. What's a little rain? She hadn't come all this way to mope about the weather.

They stopped by the only internet café in town and the cutest guy on the island approached her. Allison stuck her tongue out from across the room, making Trick giggle as he formally invited her to the Party of the Year, proclaiming he had the fastest speedboat on the island and could get them there in no time. She pointed to Allison. "My girlfriend has to come, too," she replied. He agreed, of course.

The girls went back to change their clothes into sexy dresses and gather their essentials. The rest of the group thought they were crazy because the rain was so thick you couldn't see a foot in front of you. It didn't matter to Trick and Allison. They were on a mission. They were promised the Party of the Year! They hightailed it out of there before the group's bad mojo could wear them down, but not before grabbing a black plastic bag to wrap their things in. They tied a knot in the top of the plastic bag and split.

The boat was small and fast, but not fast enough in the torrential downpour. They sat exposed, drenched, and clutching onto each other as if their very lives depended on it. Trick white-knuckled that plastic bag with the fear that if they were to go over, she could not let go of it, the realization that it would render one hand inoperable hitting her hard. They wore no life vests and that thought continued to weigh on her with every wake the boat skipped. It was a bumpy, terrifying ride that never seemed to want to end, choppy and blind as it were. Mom, I love you. Thank you for teaching me to be brave, even if you couldn't be.

They finally saw, through water-streaked eyes, a small, wooden dock. They had found the island! The boat docked and they climbed out, greeted by beautiful people not bothering with umbrellas who hurried them to safety from the storm under a wooden structure that acted as their meeting place for dining. They had erected a makeshift kitchen with the most beautiful women running it, rushing out from behind the counter to greet them and help them dry off upon their arrival. Incredibly, as soon as they got to the safety of the structure, the rain stopped. And then more people showed up. They built a bonfire between the ocean and the thick jungle behind them and pumped delicious music through an unseen sound system. People danced unabashedly.

It was almost as if it wasn't happening. Trick couldn't explain it to herself. Such bliss. A large, thick-necked man with blonde tips in his hair and a black, leather collar around his neck approached her. The collar had a leash. He handed her the end and said, "I am your slave. I will do whatever you say." She readily accepted, as it somehow made perfect sense. The guy from the speedboat had started to hover, demanding a sexual encounter as payment for driving them there. She told her slave, "Make him go away." And he did with a mere look.

One of the beauties from the kitchen with dreadlocks cascading down her back escorted her and Allison to a tent not twenty feet from the ocean break to offer them pure MDMA, for no charge at all. So easy it all was, free from external struggle and pain. The beauty's voice was sweet music to accompany the crashing waves. Trick had no idea who these people were, or where they came from. But she loved them implicitly for their tenderness and generosity. And for the rest of the night, she and Allison were free to drink, dance and be ridiculous and beautiful simultaneously. At one point, Allison was so out of her mind she nearly tried walking through the fire.

286

Trick sprinted across flames to catch her. She received no marks or burns. Unable to explain that even to herself, she wrote it off as pure magic.

When they grew weary, their hosts gave them a comfortable bed in a cabana to sleep in, with the necessary mosquito net to boot. They fell asleep in each other's arms, happy as clams.

The next morning, they made their way to the kitchen, everyone they met on the walk over sharing that knowing smile and nod. They had made it to the Party of the Year and they knew it. Best not to rub it into the faces of the others left behind upon return. They joined the other partygoers for a deliciously cooked breakfast and she got wind there was a boat sailing back to Bahia in an hour and made sure they got on it.

Trick sat by herself on the bow of the beautiful 65-foot sailboat. The day held perfect sailing conditions, with the wind at their back and a light chop, allowing everyone to sit on deck and enjoy their drinks comfortably. Soft music played throughout. Their host had kind eyes and wore white linen from head to toe. She hadn't seen him from the night before, but then, she wasn't looking. He walked through the small crowd, responding modestly to the warm reception that comes from being the Captain of the ship. He was a man comfortable in the lead. "Alright, everybody. We are now about to raise the spinnaker and get this old dame dancing!"

They cheered and he stepped forward to the gangway and asked for two volunteers to assist. He turned to Trick, "The best seat in the house is at the base of the main mast." He took her hand and guided her. After he got her comfortably situated, he directed his volunteers to drag out the spinnaker sail. The wind grabbed the sail and heaved it skyward as the boat lurched forward with speed. Glasses were raised with a roar.

Moments later, his first mate at the wheel, he returned to take the seat next to Trick. "It's customary for the skipper to make sure all of his crew know how to don their life vests. Can you save yourself, or do I have to keep my eye on you?" he winks.

"If you're hitting on me, don't. I can handle myself."

"Let's say you and I leave it in our wake. Whatever it may be," he held up his glass and she acquiesced, clinking glasses with him. "There's maybe five times a year that it's this perfect on the water. Glad you're here with me to enjoy it."

"Can we keep sailing 'til we get to the ends of the earth?"

"Let's dock, drop the rest of these freaks off, and plot our course together."

"I don't even need to pack."

"Where we're going, we won't need much," he looked at her sincerely. "I'm Guy," he said, holding out his hand.

She sized him up. She had overheard he had sailed there from Spain for this party. How bad could he be?

The sun had gone down, the others had since disembarked long before that, shouting their gratitude for a beautiful sail. Allison left with them, returning to town to tell the others they had made it out alive. Trick remained on the boat with Guy, sitting at a table for two, aglow with candlelight. The waters were dark and calm.

Guy stared at her, smiling, "I love being barefoot. I bought these deck shoes and the right one squeaks every time I walk. I'm so self-conscious every time I wear them. Sounds like I have a squeaky wheel."

"It's only fair if I get to take off my shoes, too," she said.

"I normally don't allow people on board to take their shoes off at night because it can get slick. As long as you don't you run around too much. You know what they say about the one squeaky wheel, right? It always gets oiled first."

"I'll oil you," she dared, feeling a bit frisky.

His smile widened, taking her shoes off for her. "The person who complains the most, the one who garners the most attention, gets taken care of first. I didn't want you to think I was run down."

"Time will tell."

"You know, I've always thought of sailing my boat down here and just staying. It's so quiet and peaceful. But in the end, I'd miss the big cities. Down here you feel as if you can see into the heavens. But there, everyone is busy reaching for the stars."

"Isn't that what purpose is all about? If you live on a remote island, what can you contribute to the world at large?"

"Exactly! And what could be more genuine than having a love that forms
290

an island high enough to withstand any rise of the tide? It's not about a place. The earth is always spinning. We could come here anytime we wanted, then leave whenever we got sick of it. It all starts with an us."

She was surprised by his forwardness, but liked it all the same. She felt comfortable with him. "I live hand to mouth. I've never really been in a position to give back. I have to worry about my rent, of all things. What I've always wanted to do is to make a difference in people's lives."

"We want the same things."

"I want a family."

"When do we start?"

She smiled freely.

His feet played with her feet. "I'm sure it will all appear at the right time. You did. And now I have to believe. I've been hopeful and I've lost hope. After meeting you, and where we are right now, the way this feels, I'm overjoyed that I've kept hope alive. Look at where we are because of that. We're here, together. Thank you," he smiled.

She breathed him in and closed her eyes.

10. Found

Trick woke in a large bed, surrounded by plush pillows. She slowly stirred, throwing her feet over the side of the bed and looked around the beautifully decorated room, taking in the ornate, wrought iron bedframe that looked like something out of a fairytale. Guy was not to be found. She reached down to pet her big, black and rust-colored Doberman Pinscher resting at her feet. She got up and walked out of the bedroom. The dog followed close behind, her consummate shadow.

The living room décor exuded expense, everything white. Trick rubbed sleep out of her eyes as she glided across the room in her white, silk gown. She joined her husband on the long, white couch. Guy was working on his laptop and talking on his cell phone with a cool ease about him. When she took the seat next to him, he caressed her thigh and gave her a good morning kiss to the forehead. He covered the phone with his hand and whispered, "Good morning, my love. How did you sleep?"

A satisfied smile spread across Trick's face. "Perfectly. You?"

"The best," he returned to his phone call. She rubbed his arm gently then returned to their room to dress for the day.

Emma rereads what she has written. "Contrived bullshit!!" she screams, as she deletes paragraphs by pounding on the keys of her laptop with fervor. She takes a moment to regain composure and begins typing again.

Trick is conducting a class of autistic children, kneeling down to show one student the proper way to tie his shoe. When he is able to do it himself, he claps his hands with glee as the other aides look on, smiling. She returns their smiles, beaming. She has never felt happier, more at home.

Emma stares at her laptop in disbelief. "No! That's not it! Trick's not going back to school!" she cries, highlighting the passage and deleting it quickly. She gets up and blasts some music on her stereo. She dances around the loft, swinging her arms wildly. She dances her way to the closet, changing into something appropriate for the world beyond her four walls and heads out.

She enters the gallery on a whim, having passed it a number of times and was curious what these faces looking back at her where all about. As she makes her way through the broad corridor, she sees a sign that officiates the exhibit's opening. She's very early, one of few there, and she's not unhappy about that. Crowds were not what she had in mind when she left, but neither was art. She entered on a whim.

With each passing photograph, blown up to challenge the ceiling of the massive place, she reads the passages underneath and is moved with each passing image. Young boys and girls in Africa born with cleft pallets undergoing an operation to fix their faces. Their smiles make Emma's heart shudder with emotion. The Mercy Ships were bringing aid to a land civilized society had forgotten all about. The tears flowed.

Scott Harrison, the photographer, young and handsome in jeans and dark blue blazer, approaches. He is moved by her tears, indeed they are hard to miss, and he introduces himself. She is unable to contain herself. She gushes. He receives her admiration with grace and delicately interrupts, "I want to introduce you to someone." He guides her to an area where the majority of those in attendance has convened; the focus is on a man seated behind a table signing books. Scott introduces him as the man who started the Mercy Ships. She is surprised and pleased instantly, thanking him for all of the wonderful things he has done to help facilitate goodness in this world. She is so honored to meet him and he recognizes the passion in her. He signs a book for her, inviting her to participate anytime. The door is always open.

She holds the book dear to her person, smiling her way through the newly formed crowd. A girl in her early

294

twenties, pale and mousy, sees Emma and calls out to her, "Excuse me!"

Emma turns and is greeted with a smile and a wave. She waves back at the girl, "Hello!" She approaches.

"I couldn't help noticing you, I hope you don't mind. You're a writer, right? Emma Montgomery?"

"Yes, I am."

"I read your first book! Reminded me so much of me and my brother. It was really funny!" she grins.

"Ah, yes. Back when I had a sense of humor."

"I would love to tell you about my experience with the Mercy Ships. Changed my life."

"Sure," Emma settles in.

"When I first arrived, I was given the task to go into the village to inquire about women who had been ostracized from their villages because of vaginal tearing after childbirth. Because they were not sewn up correctly, they would leak urine. And were sent away from their families because no one could stand the smell. Completely isolated. Very sad."

"That's awful."

"We would go in and find them, and invite them to have this minor surgery done, fix the tear, and reintroduce them into their villages. It was so much fun to see their faces, after taking them shopping for a new dress! Bringing them back into their homes, giving them their lives back. There's just nothing like it. Oh, the celebration was something to see!" the girl beams.

Emma laughs, "I bet. What bastards to boot them out. But I get it. Well done, sister! I can't stand hospitals and have an aversion to water. Otherwise, I'd be all over it! But I do know someone who might be interested," she offers her hand, genuinely. "Thank you for your time."

Emma begins stuffing clothes into an overnight bag. She shoves her laptop in its case, shuts off the music and lights, and heads out the door.

Chapter 10

Emma steps out of a town car, luggage in hand. The wind hits her face and whips her hair every which way. She is in Montauk, Long Island, at the estate of her dear friend and notorious photographer, Peter Beard. Swaddled in linen of various colors, he walks out barefoot to meet her on the lawn of his sprawling estate, enveloping her in a warm embrace. "You've finally taken me up on my offer, Emma. Welcome," his smile is heartfelt as he helps her with her bags into the eclectic surroundings that is his home. Photographs cover the walls, magazine piles line the floors, and lamps of foreign origin dangle disproportionately in walkways, creating a majestic glow to the cozy environment.

The sun is setting and the air smells brisk. Peter and Emma sit on the edge of a cliff of the easternmost point of Long Island, looking out onto the endless horizon. They drink red wine heartily and Peter speaks candidly. "We are all our own worst enemy. When you can figure out how to get out of your own way, the end of your book will come. What do you really want to say? Don't be a tourist. Stop treating the book so preciously and get real with it. Stay true to your characters. And get it done!" Peter grabs his camera, always at the ready, and snaps off a few shots. "Follow through is as important as a good idea."

Emma, sitting on a huge boulder and wrapped in an orange and cream striped blanket, looks beautiful and relaxed in the comfort and safety of a true artist and friend.

An hour later, a rag-tag group shows up for dinner dressed in brightly colored clothes, carrying fresh fish, garden-grown greens, and wine. There is a handsome man with bright green eyes and perfect physique that catches Emma's eye. Yet, it is the dark-skinned woman in her sixties dressed like a gypsy in her tightly fit bell-bottomed jeans and chain-metal belt and feathered headdress, commandeering the attention of the others when she speaks, that captures and keeps Emma's rapt attention. Emma is mostly taken by her carriage. She jingles with each step and reminds Emma of her mother's oldest sister, a take-no-prisoners kind of woman. Emma immediately gravitates towards her. Peter makes the introduction. "I thought you two would get on. Vanna, this is Emma. Vanna was a madame for many years. Emma's a writer. Do with that what you will," Peter half-smiles, waves a hand, and moves onward through the crowd of miscreants, forever the host. Living in such a magical place dictates his role and he owns it well.

"Lovely to meet you, sugar. A writer! Hot damn!" Vanna expresses her pleasure with only a half-glance, but the smile is there. She heads into the kitchen, much left to prepare for the feast at hand.

Later, Emma moves closer to her, side-sliding smooth-like around the long, wooden table. The two women size each other up worldlessly, with a modicum of eye-ball prying. The battle of silent willfulness engaged,

298

they allow the relaxed atmosphere the satisfaction from a good meal provides, to shed any bravado. It is not necessary, what with infinity as their immediate horizon. This is not the place to try to be anything you are not, deciding instead on a playful embrace with the warmth only an invitation of a close friend who knows you best can deliver. A litmus test, if you will. All goodness here. Emma is struck by Vanna's scent: musky oil that reminds her of what railroad car-hopping would smell like plus french pastries peppered with the promise of adventure. She loves her further.

Most of the guests wander off to take in the expansive grounds at night with panoramic views of the profoundly impossible black infinity. Emma follows this beautiful, brown gypsy into the living room like an obedient puppy. Vanna chooses to sit, Indian style, on the floor, her bells splayed, and begins to hold court to the few gathered around her. She is someone who has clearly seen it all. Tough to the bone, yet sweet and soft as a lullaby. Vanna is beautiful to Emma.

Everyone is in their zone, moving smoothly to the music piped into the house's sound system seamlessly, the cadence of which can best be described as milky fluidity, a nice compliment to the art surrounding their heads. Images of gorgeous, other-wordly models photographed in the wilds of Africa, smeared with Peter's touches, albeit blood or whatever, every bit captivating. All of it making sense, everyone knowing that this brand of art, perchance constricting with its severity, is where they are now, and they love where they are now, nowhere they'd rather be. The sheer stillness outside is immeasurable. Best to stay close and ponder life's mysteries. Vanna has many fans.

The music hums and the beats reach lower level. Those who haven't wandered off in search of the mindless, ultimate reset button, mingle. When Emma finally gets the chance to pry Vanna from the others and speak to her, in her excitement, she does so delicately and deliberately, "Vanna, may I talk to you about your experiences as a madame? I'm writing a book about the sex trade and..." She hears her own voice and cringes. But then, she's never been accused of being subtle. Fuck it, she thinks. What do I have to lose. I have a book to finish.

"How were you traveling with the sex trade industry?" Vanna booms.

"I wasn't. But my path crossed with some women who were. And are currently," she hedges.

"What do you want to write about, Sugar? You going into detail of money exchanges and for what act? Are the girls working the stroll? Are they in regular massage parlors? Are the escorts through a service in ads? Are they by word of mouth? Or bar girls? Do they work for nude encounters in bookstores? Possibly by contract, like Bunny Ranch? Independent contractors? Or do they just give it up for promotions? Corner girls? Do you go into detail the many million different acts a program can entail?" Vanna has ripped attention from the fabric of the room and directed it towards her near tirade.

300

"It's a... a bit more intimate than that. One girl carving out her place in that world," Emma stammers.

"There certainly are millions of working girls all with completely different stories and outcomes."

"Of course. Well, this girl is almost destroyed by it."

"Please don't believe the hype that all working girls do so because of bad childhood or rape. That's crap. People look down on them so this makes them more acceptable through pity. It is amazing to me! Whores, or is it hoes now? There are more free-fucking hoes in this world that are just giving it away! Don't worry about health because he's the one! Oh heavens! Come and get it. Free pussy! Promise me a second date, of course I'll suck your dick without a rubber. Now, these are the pitiful women."

"She got into the wrong scene and the drugs took a real toll on her."

"There's a lot of blaming booze. I never did a client with drugs or booze. I owned seven parlors in six states and no one used anything. Ever. I've seen ladies who were being controlled by pimps. This is one type of human life that had to stay the fuck away from me and mine. They drink in strip joints because the business makes all the big money off of champagne. Also, many girls have big fun in that lifestyle. But the booze and cogs and the lines etcetera catch up to everyone. Makes it easier to let others into your wallet. In my places, no boyfriend or pimp was ever allowed on my property. No phone calls or no man stopping in to drop

301

off food or score money from the girls. That way the girl has time not only to do her job in a happier frame of mind, but also has time to think or study. Plus, your regular clientele don't want to see some creep hanging around!" Vanna snaps.

Emma explains it's more of a coming into oneself kind of story, a work of fiction based on the lives of several sex trade workers she spoke to. She tells Vanna she has grown to respect the choices of these young women she based her character Trick on, without judgment, because they owned their choices even if it caused them harm at times. "These girls learned from putting themselves out there and if anything," Emma explains, "I'm fascinated by their bravery." She offers to read a passage from her book to Vanna and the others, because why not, she thinks. If this woman hates it, I'm still publishing it. It would be nice to have her blessing, but still. Time to give it wings.

She takes out her laptop and reads a passage, "... This hypocrisy belies professional gals their reason to boast because it is in this condemnation these brave girls, who have grown into women warriors, find their full voice, laugh out loud and often, dress as outrageous birds, feel the most alive, and at their very best remain untouchable."

"Send it, baby!" Vanna says in her signature booming voice, inhabiting the whole of the space that is the living room. The others clap their hands.

"Send it!" a voice in the back of the room shouts, accompanying the applause.

302

"See, Darling? Your fans are waiting!" Vanna laughs and it feels like the whole house shakes.

Emma is pleased to receive her blessing, but something is still bothering her. "Vanna? I killed off her mother and I feel terrible about it ever since. Why did I do that? I think I thought it was the only real way to save her from herself."

"Dear, I speak to my mother daily. Don't take away her foundation. It's not necessary. You don't need a sacrificial lamb to save Trick. She doesn't need saving! She's fine just the way she is," Vanna's smile could light up the night sky.

"Thank you. I needed to hear that," Emma says, and wraps her arms around this big, colorful woman, who returns the hug, deeply.

Emma returns later that night to her quarters, one of Peter's numerous small guesthouses. There's a tiny bed, an antique wooden desk, and a lamp with a dim bulb. She sets up her laptop and takes a seat. The sound of bleating goats can be heard outside the open window next to the desk where Emma is typing away feverishly.

10. Found

Trick heard the sound of his classic show truck and secretly hoped he brought goodies. She had just gotten off

303

the phone with her mother, sharing the news of the day and scoffing, a certain respite to her every day, and she needed a few moments to herself. She scanned the room to make sure nothing was left out of place. The lights were dimmed just so, mirrors hidden from view. She didn't need the distraction. At this age, she knew her beauty still beamed from the inside out.

Morris was a real genius, a chemical engineer, and her client for the last nine years. She saw him every Monday and Thursday and for three hours, they would watch a program on tv, or football during season, then sit and talk. She always enjoyed how passionately he spoke about his dogs that he loved and was content to be his shoulder to lean on when he griped about his wife, whom he hated. He'd grown sick of his wife's threats, so he stayed married to her until he, in his own words, murdered her. He had no interest in sharing his wealth and beloved pets, in the case of a divorce settlement, with a woman who had made his life a living hell for the last thirty years.

He found comfort with Trick. The two hours of stimulating conversation was enough foreplay to then knock off a chunk and hug. She had adopted long ago
304

that there would be no drinking and never drugs, as well as no kissing or exchange of any bodily fluids. That kept things sorted in her mind. She came to value her trade tremendously over the years, but her safety, both physically and emotionally, came first. Plus, she appreciated the arrangement because using substances wasn't an option anymore - it fogged her judgment for too many years and had made her feel like a sitting duck. If she ever let a client feel like they had gotten too close, to allow herself to feel soft in the presence of a client, especially her single ones, she wouldn't be able to stand the constant attention from any one of them thinking they had something "real" with her. Her privacy, earning power, and personal space was paramount to her success after all these years. Falling in love was a thing of the distant past and she refused any advances otherwise. She had missed the love boat and had come to terms with it long ago. She got enough of what she needed from these men. And her mother was always there to pick up the slack, to talk about the things unspoken to others, without judgment, accepting each other as they were with secrets reserved for the one that never came.

Instead, they found that brand of solace in each other. Soul mates come in all forms.

The women around her were the throwbacks of society, the products of broken marriages, hearts, and homes. Still, they could laugh. Trick grew very protective of the other girls living at the motel. She had seen enough through the years and knew deep down what all women want to feel: safe. She was their protector.

When a client was generous enough to buy her groceries, she always bought extra to hand out to the other girls. She knew what they liked. Once, the woman living in the room behind her took to beating her child, a bastard from a client who disappeared on her. The very next day, Trick told her that if she ever laid hands on him again, she would kill her. That put an end to that.

She helped others with everyday errands, driving people where they needed to go because her eyesight was still 20/20 and her hearing was surprisingly good, despite all the deafening music she had danced to for so many years in so many clubs, all those late nights. She had her memories to make her smile.

It was a good, calm life. Not what she had expected, but then, she had to let go of expectations long ago. She felt that she could have done more. At one point, she had wanted to save the world. But we will do what we will and no one can convince us otherwise. Nothing limiting about doing what you do best.

She gave back in her own way, making others feel adored and appreciated. Her redemption in their acceptance of what she had to offer was gold bars. In that, Trick never felt happier. Her mother had never tried to be or prove anything to anyone, and now neither was she. These women knew their worth. She learned to abhor stress and cut it at the quick. Her opting out of marriage with children had brought her temporary grief. But then, children are so much work. She chose, instead, to embrace her divine skillset to provide pleasure and comfort to others and remained thoroughly resolute as her own work in progress.

The new day breaks. Emma, bleary-eyed and hunched over, types the last of it. She sits back and stares at the screen, zoned. She slowly closes her laptop, climbs into the little bed, beneath a pile of covers, and crashes. Hard.

Epilogue

New York Times best-selling author for a second time, Emma Montgomery, sits at a table in a bookstore, surrounded by copies of her new novel *Mistaken For Trash*. There are people milling about with her book in their hands. Others wait patiently a line to meet the author.

A distraught, yet gentle woman walks up to the table. "Hi! My husband committed suicide three weeks ago. He loved your work. Can you sign it in loving memory of Hank?" she rubs her aging hands together.

Emma smiles at her gently. "I'm sorry to hear that. At least he's no longer in pain," she signs. The woman nods her head and thanks her.

A man approaches the table. "Hello, Ms. Montgomery. I lost a daughter. She left home early. Maybe if she reads this she'll come home?" he pauses and takes a breath. "I know where you're coming from. Can you write it to my other daughter, her twin, the one I still have? Her name is Sharon."

"Of course," she replies. Emma eyes him carefully before signing. He takes his book and leaves.

The woman right behind him steps up, speaking quickly. "Thank you! What a difficult, but beautiful book! You must be so proud. I've never done anything in my life. Whatever you want to write would be inspirational. I've always wanted to be a writer!" she beams.

Emma takes a deep breath. She squares her shoulders and writes, "Thank you. I'm free! Warmest, Trick." Emma puts down her pen, closes her eyes, and smiles.

www.ingramcontent.com/pod-product-compliance
Lightning Source LLC
Chambersburg PA
CBHW020350110726
47899CB00006B/1663